The
Comic
Style
of
Beaumarchais

The Comic Style of Beaumarchais

BY J. B. RATERMANIS AND W. R. IRWIN

GREENWOOD PRESS, PUBLISHERS
NEW YORK

*Published with the assistance of a grant from the
Graduate College of the State University of Iowa*

Preface

In discussions of comedy two extremes of error often occur: one a loose and irresponsible appreciation, the other a pedantic worrying of the text which goes far toward justifying the popular notion that nothing is so wearisome as laughter explained. It is not easy to avoid either of these errors. The delights of well-executed comedy might tempt almost any responsive reader to raptures; the richness of elements which are fused in a single unsurpassable comic exchange or in a work of sustained excellence is an invitation to exhausting analysis. Yet the critic who errs in either way does a disservice to comedy, just as the sentimentalist or the precisian, whatever his motives, injures true religion.

We have tried in this essay not only to shun these extremes but also to focus on *Le Barbier de Séville* and *Le Mariage de Figaro* a scrutiny flexible enough to match the variety of Beau-

marchais' wit, yet precise and principled enough to produce a
cohesive interpretation of his work. The method which we propose to follow is set forth briefly, but we trust adequately, in
the Introduction. No one should expect of this a full theory of
comedy or even a formulary statement of all the generalizations which we have found applicable to Beaumarchais. Rather
we intend the Introduction as a presentation of some crucial
definitions and a preliminary statement of principles which will
be exemplified throughout our analyses of the two plays. The
careful reader will also notice that in the discussion of *Le
Mariage de Figaro* the number of passages detailedly examined
diminishes. This does not at all mean that we consider Beaumarchais' second comedy an impoverished work. Rather we
believe that the reader himself will, as he continues, become
accustomed to our method almost to the point of applying it
himself, and may properly find more interest in our discussion
of the complexities which make this play a rich, though somewhat disorderly, expression of comic genius.

A reader totally unacquainted with *Le Barbier de Séville* and
Le Mariage de Figaro would benefit little from what we have
written. A familiarity with the operatic adaptations of Rossini
and Mozart would be helpful, despite the artistic independence
which may validly be claimed for these works. Best of all, of
course, would be a fresh and thorough knowledge of Beaumarchais' texts. Even so, this is not a book solely for special-
ists in Beaumarchais, eighteenth-century French comedy, or
general dramaturgy. The theory of comedy and its application
cannot be child's play, but we see no reason for it to be eso-
teric or complicated beyond the intellectual control of the
common reader, as this felicitous phrase has been understood
since Dr. Johnson used it. Accordingly, we believe that our
work will be intelligible to anyone who can read colloquial
French prose with a quick response to its connotations. For
those who wish to consider further details of Beaumarchais'
style, especially for insight into the development of his texts
from a crude to a finished form, we have made the notes as
full as they can be without becoming unwieldy. But we believe
that those who wish can follow our analysis without reference
to them.

A word is perhaps pertinent on the title which we chose,

having weighed and rejected many. We understand "style" in a widely inclusive sense. For our purposes it is more than proper words in proper places and certainly more than the literary manifestation of Beaumarchais' personality. In this study "style" comprehends, in addition to the usual aspects of manner with language, the interplay of character, action, and expression, in their dramatic significations.

We wish to express our gratitude for advice and suggestions to Professors Edmund de Chasca and Frederick P. W. McDowell of the State University of Iowa, and to the late Walter F. Loehwing, Dean of the Graduate College, for grants in support of the research and publications.

J. B. Ratermanis
W. R. Irwin

Contents

1. *Introduction*   3

2. *Le Barbier de Séville*   12

3. *Le Mariage de Figaro*   49

4. *Conclusion*   109

Notes   121

Bibliography   139

The
Comic
Style
of
Beaumarchais

·1·

Introduction

Pierre Augustin Caron de Beaumarchais attempted to revive the comic spirit in France from a worse than languishing condition. It is a familiar fact of literary history that Paris as well as London during the eighteenth century saw a long and disheartening "déclin de la gaîté théâtrale," conspicuous for following a period of brilliant achievement in comedy. In both nations the persistent causes of decline were twofold: the increasing fondness of theatrical managers and of the public for subrational entertainment—Italian opera, harlequinades, spectacles (often starring animals), buffoonery, low farce, and others; and the infiltration of sentimentality, which brought with it bourgeois tragedy, melodrama, and the abused but durable *comédie larmoyante*. Against all these innovations French and English dramatists, critics, and theater lovers complained energetically but for long with little success. This was an un-

happy period in the history of two great national theaters, and
its general course is well enough known to require no detailed
tracing here[1]

Beaumarchais several times commented on the sad state of
the contemporary stage and on his attempts to improve it, but
the following statement in his preface to *Le Mariage de Figaro*
may be taken as a summary of his diagnosis and his claim:

> J'ai donc réfléchi que si quelque homme courageux ne secouait pas
> toute cette poussière, bientôt l'ennui des Pièces françaises porte-
> rait la nation au frivole Opéra-Comique, et plus loin encore, aux
> Boulevards, à ce ramas infect de tréteaux élevés à notre honte, où la
> décente liberté, bannie du Théâtre français, se change en une licence
> effrénée, où la jeunesse va se nourrir de grossières inepties, et
> perdre, avec ses moeurs, le goût de la décence et des chefs-d'oeuvres
> de nos maîtres. J'ai tenté d'être cet homme, et si je n'ai pas mis
> plus de talent à mes ouvrages, au moins mon intention s'est-elle
> manifestée dans tous.[2]

Time and mature critical opinion have little altered Beaumarchais' indictment of the theatrical practices which he faced.
There is some debate over the efficacy of his attempted remedy. Be this as it may, his effort to reform produced two
comedies whose fame, which was both immediate and persistent, leads us to believe that they embody qualities essentially
comic, qualities which have remained unchangingly effective
through the changes of literary development and taste. We hope
that this essential can be isolated—or perhaps only suggested—
through a careful study of what we call the comic style of Beaumarchais.

At the outset we may properly specify several kinds of in-
vestigation which will have no prominent part in this essay.
Historians of literature have so clearly shown Beaumarchais'
place in the contemporary scene and his affiliations with pre-
cursors that those need not be detailed here. It is equally well
known that Beaumarchais was significantly influenced by the
ideology of Diderot. He himself acknowledged the debt,[3] which
is evident even in the comedies. But since we shall be concerned with analysis of comic style in his two major plays, we
shall accordingly ignore their sentimental and propagandist
aspects, as well as the personal reasons which impelled him
to this kind of expression. Nor will it be much to our purpose

to trace the growth of his two comedies, though from time to time reference to line variations in earlier versions will illuminate important modifications in action, characterization, dialogue, or total *vis comica*.

Though possible sources of Beaumarchais' plays have been ably traced by Eugène Lintilhac, [4] precise analysis of the comic mechanisms in the works themselves has scarcely been attempted. Even in an intensive study of Beaumarchais, Félix Gaiffe does not venture beyond general impressions. Thus, for example, he characterizes the intrigues:

> . . . intrigue savamment combinée et franchement gaie, la rapidité des incidents, l'ingéniosité des combinaisons, l'imprévu des situations, la virtuosité avec laquelle l'auteur semble à chaque instant engager ses personnages dans une impasse pour les en tirer d'un coup de baguette magique. . . [5]

Though entirely accurate, this description might with equal justice be applied to the action of any one of a number of comedies and even to parts of some melodramas. The contribution of the intrigue to comic effect remains undefined.

A similar deficiency may be seen in Gaiffe's discussion of characters. We are told, again with reason, that gaiety sparkles in each retort:

> . . . la gaîté étincelait à chaque réplique; le Comte, Figaro, Rosine, sont pétillants d'allègre jeunesse, Bartholo et Bazile nous divertissent à leurs dépens, mais non sans esprit, et si l'on peut reprocher à cet esprit d'être celui de l'auteur, on ne peut s'empêcher de rire, quand le mot plaisant part comme une fusée. [6]

But again something like precision is needed, and—more important—some insight into the specifically comic qualities of the verbal interplay.

The failings noted above are by no means owing to Gaiffe's ineptitude. Rather they are only symptomatic of a paucity of close critical studies of the comic style of individual authors and their works. Of all the great comic writers of France only Molière has been more or less adequately examined in this respect. Even those critics who profess or reveal an interest in the effects of comedy appear unwilling to wrestle with the protean subject of its mechanisms until its secret is extorted.

It is a simple fact that there is no universally accepted explanation for comic effect, in literature or in life. We cannot hope to review here all of the proposed explanations or even the prominent aspects of the prominent theories. Moreover, there could be no assurance that the conclusions from so comprehensive a rehearsal would be worth more than any one critical thesis. We prefer therefore to determine the common features of several currently reputable theories which seem to pertain most clearly to the two major works of Beaumarchais. Even if our choice of theories is arbitrary—and it is, since we have purposely ignored, for example, all theories which make comedy a function of ethics—these common characteristics have some chance of corresponding to the realities of the comic as it is manifest in the work of Beaumarchais.

It is generally conceded that laughter in response to artistic representation is impossible without certain conditions favorable to the one who laughs. Beaumarchais himself points out that for the enjoyment of comedy one must be, for the time, free of care, for "on rit peu de la gaieté d'autrui, quand on a de l'humeur pour son propre compte. . . ."[7] This implies that any comic work relies on some detachment from the troublesome involvements of life. Clearly, this detachment results in part from the reader's or spectator's comfort—"content de votre santé, de vos affaires, de votre Maîtresse, de votre dîner, de votre estomac"—, from his willing suspension of anxiety, and in part from the play's effectiveness in diverting his attention from his daily preoccupations. In any case, laughter presupposes release from all strong emotion, and requires serenity or at least a reduced tension, analogous perhaps to that of a dream.[8] One of our tasks will be to determine how fully the two comedies of Beaumarchais conform to these important, though somewhat negative, conditions.

It is much more difficult to select from the many proposals offered those characteristics of comedy which positively account for artistically stimulated laughter. This is the task which Charles Lalo undertook. He suggested a grouping of all theories of the comic into two classes: those relying on contrast, whereby laughter is a response to some opposition, contradiction, incongruity, or absurdity; and those which discern degradation, so that laughter is an expression of disparagement or censorious negation. In the last formulation laughter establishes the superiority—the "sudden glory" which Thomas

Hobbes emphasized—of the one who laughs over the object of his amusement.[9] According to Lalo, most such theories have some validity, although not all degradation, any more than every instance of absurd contrast, is to be regarded as comic.

Even so, comic contrast is, according to the theorists, diverse rather than uniform. Some, particularly Kant and his successors, see it as a series of sentiments which exclude or oppose each other, such as expectation of great events which show themselves on realization to be insignificant. Others maintain that comic contrast is essentially intellectual or logical. This is the thesis of Marc Chapiro in *L'Illusion comique* (1940), Elie Aubouin in *La Technique et psychologie du comique* (1948) and, to a certain extent, of Max Eastman in *The Enjoyment of Laughter* (1936). Chapiro believes that comic laughter is provoked by an absurd representation which is momentarily accepted because it is concealed behind a "mask," that is, some specious justification or demonstration, as, for example, that two plus two equals five. The comic, then, is a transient illusion, which frees us from the oppressive ascendance of reality, and laughter an expression of liberty.[10] The over-all process is much the same for Aubouin. He holds that comic laughter is stimulated by "la conciliation ludique de deux inconciliables."[11] Again the justification can only be specious and can satisfy no more than our propensity for playfulness. Further, this "conciliation ludique" bears upon the form only, not the content, of the representation, and thus constitutes a kind of superfluous activity.

The two just mentioned belong to the so-called intellectualist theories of comedy. Lalo observes that these criteria for the comic—liberation, playfulness, illusion—actually pertain to art in general and are not distinctive features of comedy, though they may be seen with unusual clarity in this genre. Thus the intellectualist thesis leaves a need for a fuller explanation of comic contrast. For analogous reasons Lalo rejects a general application of the well-known formula of Henri Bergson, though he readily acknowledges its value as a partial explanation. Lalo maintains that to see the source of laughter only in "le mécanique plaqué sur du vivant" is to miss the effective component. Moreover, there are instances cited by Bergson himself in which the comic seems to result from an exactly contrary procedure; life is grafted upon the mechanical and interferes with it. [12] Even Bergson's jack-in-the-box can be thought a mechanical object on which a kind of living energy has been imposed. Nonetheless, Bergson's is still a theory of contrast, even though limited in its application by the vitalist philosophy on which it is based.

Lalo himself attempts a definition sufficiently comprehensive to include every comic situation. He seeks to escape the limitations of other theories by joining the two aspects, contrast and degradation, which others have recognized but mistakenly separated. "Entre ces manifestations, si différentes à divers égards, la donnée qui reste commune, c'est *une dissonance, résolue par en bas, entre deux ou plusieurs valeurs contre-pointées;* ou, d'un mot, *une dévaluation.*" [13] Elsewhere he summarizes thus: "*Contraste + Dégradation = Dévaluation,* telle est l'équation du rire esthétique" (p. 33). By *valeur* Lalo, orthodoxly enough, means the object of individual or social desire, and presumably there is some value implicit in every object or idea. It follows then that, except for absolute values in a given society, it is possible to laugh at anything or anybody.

The synoptic observations which precede permit us to adopt as a working hypothesis the following points of general agreement: (1) nothing is laughable in itself, but anything can become so; (2) the comic cannot exist without contrast or opposition of some kind; (3) this contrast, whatever its nature, is normally masked, that is, speciously justified and thus accepted, or resolved, though in respect to form only; (4) a rational pleasure is associated with and sought in the act of laughter.

Opinions vary as to the nature and cause of this last component. In our opinion the most plausible explanation is again Lalo's, inasmuch as his concept of value is applicable to all possible cases. Comic laughter, he maintains, disturbs the normal sense of harmony which derives from the acceptance of conventional values, and this diversion produces a momentary surprise and pleasure, both rational, that distinguish the comic arts from all others. It may also leave a more or less permanent sharpening of the critical faculty, but this is an increment beyond the immediate response.

It does not follow from the preceding paragraphs that we

feel detailedly bound to Lalo's theory or to that of any other critic. We are rather in general accord with the intellectualist approach as amplified by Lalo and Aubouin. The reader will not be surprised, then, if in our analysis we relegate the affective aspect of the comic to second place. In the examination which we propose the important concepts are expressed in the terms *dévaluation, dégradation, masque, conciliation,* and most of all *contraste.* It seems inescapable that every comic situation is characterized by duality, more or less overt. From this we conclude that search through all possible variations for contrast and resolution must be our principal effort.

Yet a problem remains. How may these general theories, all requiring cautious use, be applied to the highly individual works of Beaumarchais? We are not concerned with showing that Beaumarchais subscribed to a precise formulation, or that any one theory is more valid than another. Rather we wish to reveal the means by which Beaumarchais filled and vitalized what, when stated generally, is only an abstract frame. We wish to note, of course, what genuinely comic elements in his plays are outside that of contrast, inclusive though this concept is. Even more, we hope to show Beaumarchais' skill in incorporating highly diversified contrast into the unity of a work of dramatic art designed for spectators and readers not for the most part preoccupied with the theory of comedy. Thus we propose to sketch the dominant features of the comic style of Beaumarchais. Much will necessarily be omitted or slighted, particularly what is contributed to the whole by purely stage effects. Even so, we hope to define his style, convinced that style, understood inclusively, is the gold of the treasure which the comic artist offers to all who will accept it.

We owe our readers an explanation of some other terms which, though often ambiguous, can scarcely be avoided. These are wit, irony, and humor. Aubouin devoted an entire work, *Les Genres du risible* (1948), to the discrimination of such key concepts. In general we shall assign to the terms the meanings which Aubouin gives them, and it should be noted that these will vary slightly from normal English usage, particularly in connotation. Thus by "wit," which pertains most to the intelligence, we signify the process of discovering unexpected oppositions or identifications of contrary elements in the domain of ideas and words. It is through wit that comic conciliation can be achieved logically. Irony is a particular form of wit in which there is a calculated discrepancy between what is said and what is meant. Irony heightens the comic effect when it superficially reconciles absurdity and sense. Humor consists in the assimilation of contradictory sentiments provoked by a single object or event. Humor transcends blame and approval, and its area of relevance comprehends both logicality and absurdity. Bergson and Raymond Bayer[14] stressed the predominance of the concrete in humor. Be this as it may, the breadth and tolerance of humor make it properly described as the comic become contemplative.

Aubouin also distinguishes between the comic and the ridiculous, though the two are often found in close conjunction. The latter implies censure or derision of behavior incompatible with a norm; it provokes the laughter of rejection. The comic, however, does not exclude compassion, and only the comic can carry with it a specious, sometimes whimsical, justification. The ridiculous pretendedly justified becomes the comic.

We recognize, of course, that distinctions among these aspects are easy enough in theoretical discourse but difficult often to discern in specific analysis. Therefore we shall not attempt to maintain them rigorously in scrutinizing the work of Beaumarchais. Rather we shall limit ourselves to indicating one aspect or another as predominant in specific passages and parts under examination. Temperament or taste may safely be allowed latitude in these instances; to be rigid is to fall into the vanity of dogmatizing. But the feature of the comic which is uniform and resists idiosyncratic interpretation is the prevalence of contrast leading to the justified or resolved contradiction.

We shall avoid another, indeed a time-honored, categorization, which divides the artistic whole into the comedy of character, of manners, of situation, of words, and of gestures. This system of distinction superficially resembles what we have already developed, in that comedy of character, manners, and situation roughly belong to the comic and the ridiculous, while comedy of words is a manifestation of wit. Even so, these standard divisions seem to us unsatisfying. Once it is conceded that the essential comic mechanism is a constant,

this classification seems highly artificial when compared with
one which respects the different orders of the comic, arranged
according to the psychic and emotional responses which they
stimulate.

It is, however, important that we accept another distinction
often noted by theoreticians of comedy. Not all laughter is aesthetic. The laughters of good health, of release after tension,
or of simple happiness are—from an artistic though not from
a natural point of view—"parasite" laughter. But they promote
aesthetic response, perhaps by a kind of catalysis, and no
comic author—certainly not Beaumarchais—would neglect them.
Again it is easier to separate the two in theoretical statement
than in direct analysis of passages.

We believe, of course, that within any period of historically
developing taste there is substantial agreement as to what does
and what does not create a comic effect. Indeed, meaningful
discussion of any aesthetic problem requires some assumption
of consensus. Likely it is true, as Lalo suggests, that we laugh
otherwise than did our ancestors. That is, we laugh for much
the same reasons, but with a different application of these
reasons,[15] since the system of references for any pair of contrasted values has perhaps changed. Nonetheless, the operation
of contrast itself remains, and from it one half of the pair still
suffers devaluation, even if historic values have undergone
reversal. It is only the degree of devaluation and its immediate
significance which are inconstant. Through changing society
and taste there exist permanent principles for literary evocation of laughter, and it is one manifestation of these which we
hope to discover in examining the comic style of Beaumarchais.

·2·

Le Barbier
de Seville

Accepting the usual assumption, we take the principal operative
components in a comedy to be characters, action, and verbal
expression. These are, of course, distinguishable, and we
shall, as we deem necessary, concentrate now on one, now on
another. But an analysis which leaves these elements separate
is at best incomplete and more likely misleading. Accordingly,
our over-all effort will be to show the interplay of characters,
action, and expression, for not only does each component contribute to the others, but the three fuse to maintain the unity
of both of Beaumarchais' comedies as they run their course
from beginning to end.

Act I

In the brief opening monologue the Count Almaviva suggests
his own part in the play and the focus of the entire action. He is

a type of the sophisticated lover—self-conscious, a bit jaded with success, an amiable, harmless Don Giovanni. He varies little from this role, and his contribution to comic effect is accordingly limited, though real enough.

He first sees Figaro, his intrepid ally-servant, as a distraction from his sudden consuming passion. The song which Figaro is composing is, to be sure, little in harmony with a lover's rhapsodic banalities. It contributes nothing to the action. But it does appropriately introduce Figaro as the main character, and it creates a much-needed disposition to laughter. Figaro is no hero of romance: wine is his servant, laziness his mistress, and pleasure his god. The doctrine is disreputable, but the professor so graceful that he recommends himself at once. His song and his ensuing conversation with the count clearly establish his dominant traits: humorous detachment and wit. [1] These combine with his energy to make Figaro the principal source of the comic as well as the prime mover for the success of the count's desires.

Beaumarchais found it convenient, for purposes of exposition, to impose upon these old acquaintances the necessity of renewing their intimacy after a long separation. Momentarily Figaro is deceived by the count's disguise. After an odd bit of dialogue in which each man is talking to himself, recognition comes quickly, and in the exchange which follows is the beginning of their successful alliance. The lines deserve close analysis, for their revelation of external personal characteristics and even more for the comic effects of language which emerge from them.

Figaro. —. . . Cet air altier et noble. . . .
Le Comte. —Cette tournure grotesque. . . .
Figaro. —Je ne me trompe point; c'est le Comte Almaviva.
Le Comte. —Je crois que c'est ce coquin de Figaro.
Figaro. —C'est lui-même, Monseigneur.
Le Comte. —Maraud! si tu dis un mot. . . .
Figaro. —Oui, je vous reconnais; voilà les bontés familières dont
    vous m'avez toujours honoré. (I, 2)

The combination here of parallel syntax and phrasing with contrasted terms makes for rapid pace and markedly comic effects. "Altier et noble" is balanced by "tournure grotesque." The exclamation "c'est le Comte Almaviva" is followed im-

mediately by "c'est ce coquin de Figaro. " "Monseigneur" is
matched with "maraud. " The count deals here in somewhat un-
imaginative scorn, and Figaro seemingly consents to his own
degradation, indeed promotes it by replying to "coquin" with
the honorific title "monseigneur. " He only pretends to accept
the insult attached to his name: actually all he acknowledges is
the name itself. And in his next speech he is able to return the
insult by suggesting that abuse of his dependents is a distinctive
feature of the count's manners. The count tries to recoup with
"si gros et si gras, " and Figaro's response, "c'est la misère, " gives direction to the remainder of the scene.

The contrast between the count's description (including his
phrase "tournure grotesque") and the suffering which Figaro
claims, creates an absurdity: Figaro has grown fat on woe.
Somewhat like Falstaff, Figaro is able to enjoy amusement at
his own expense, as the count never could. He is aware that
his appearance belies the pathetic tale he is about to relate.
Yet relate it he will and will moreover make the scornful master glad to take him back into service. Figaro's recurrent
readiness to depreciate himself to serve his own ends is a result of his fundamentally detached view of life.

After the briefest possible mention of present business the
dialogue returns to Figaro's woeful past:

Le Comte. – . . . Eh bien, cet emploi?
Figaro. – Le Ministre, ayant égard à la recommandation de Votre
    Excellence, me fit nommer sur-le-champ Garçon Apothicaire.
Le Comte. –Dans les hôpitaux de l'Armée?
Figaro. –Non; dans les haras d'Andalousie. (I, 2)

Two scales of value are opposed in "excellence" and "garçon
apothicaire. " The count's dignity is somewhat impaired simply
by association with an apprentice, even more by the fact that
his puissant word had but a trivial result. Even worse for the
count, his protégé was trusted not with wounded soldiers but
with horses only. The passage has, however, a purpose beyond
the discomfiture of the count. By the degrading assimilation of
man to horse, an identification stressed by the alliteration of
"armée" and "haras, " not only the devaluation of the count is
effected, but of the government, and perhaps of the race of men

in general. And the unexpectedness of Figaro's final line only
emphasizes the satirical coup.

The continuing dialogue introduces further complexity:

Le Comte. —Beau début!

Figaro. —Le poste n'était pas mauvais; parce qu'ayant le district des
   pansements et des drogues, je vendais souvent aux hommes de
   bonnes médecines de cheval. . . .

Le Comte. —Qui tuaient les sujets du Roi!

Figaro. —Ah! Ah! il n'y a point de remède universel; mais qui n'ont
   pas laissé de guérir quelquefois des Galiciens, des Catalans,
   des Auvergnats. (I, 2)

The identification of man and horse persists, now based on
their having received the same dosage from the enterprising
Figaro. Into this ironical contrast is introduced the opposition
of "tuer" and "guérir, " an opposition which is eventually reconciled. The count voices the reproach which one might expect
of his conventionality. Again, Figaro seems to acknowledge it,
only to justify himself in the same sentence. The equation of
man and horse here acts as a "mask" for Figaro's disingenuousness.

The passage contains another identification, "sujets du Roi"
with "Galiciens, " "Catalans, " "Auvergnats. " Figaro is in
effect declaring that a large part of the population benefited
from horse tonic. Thus his acceptance of the count's reproach
is scarcely heartfelt. Really Figaro asserts that what is good
for the horse is good for its master. The reader's understanding of this spectacular impertinence is delayed, unexpected,
and therefore the more laughable.

Yet another interpretation is possible. Figaro's "il n'y a
point de remède universel" is simply a recognition of the fact
that many "sujets du Roi" died of his ministrations. These do
not much interest him. But the tough peasant group may be
admired for its horselike hardiness. According to F. H. Osgood, this is a city jibe at provincials.[2] Perhaps it is, though
the audience's unfamiliarity with these particular rural groups
limits the appeal of the joke. It is noteworthy that in American
vaudeville skits, towns named as exemplars of provinciality
were usually not obscure villages but well-known small cities
set in rural areas, such as Dubuque, Peoria, Topeka. Even

so, many will laugh at the suggestion that any group of human beings, no matter how credulous or robust, can thrive on the medications of a horse doctor. If it seems that Beaumarchais' joking on misplaced veterinary effort is far removed from the present action, one must remember that Bartholo, the chief antagonist, though yet unseen, prides himself unwontedly on being a member of the medical profession.

Meanwhile, Figaro has not explained his presence in Seville. In doing so he takes the reader again into a part of his past:

Voilà précisément la cause de mon malheur, Excellence. Quand on a rapporté au Ministre que je faisais, je puis dire assez joliment, des bouquets à Cloris; que j'envoyais des énigmes aux Journaux; qu'il courait des Madrigaux de ma façon; en un mot, quand il a su que j'étais imprimé tout vif, il a pris la chose au tragique, et m'a fait ôter mon emploi, sous prétexte que l'amour des Lettres est incompatible avec l'esprit des affaires. (I, 2)

The ornate pastoral style from an apprentice apothecary, as well as the ambitions incommensurate with his station, create a fantasy personality, such as is described by Max Eastman, in which irreconcilables are factitiously blended. These very pretensions moved a no doubt conscientious *ministre* to discharge Figaro, or in the language of comic theory, to suppress the duality. Characteristically, Figaro finds this not at all surprising; it is the fate of unappreciated genius.

Two euphemisms, "amour des lettres" and "esprit des affaires," stand in conspicuous contrast. The reason attributed to the minister is patently absurd, and Figaro's repetition of his language is, of course, ironic. Actually, Figaro will soon prove himself an agile man of affairs, but the two phrases in conjunction present a cliché of common prejudice. It is one of the effects of Figaro's personality to negate the wisdom of mediocrity; one cannot judge a virtuoso by the standards of bureaucracy. In recognizing the minister's limitations the count adopts momentarily an irony resembling his servant's: "Puissamment raisonné! Et tu ne lui fis pas représenter. . . . "But Figaro pushes on with an epigram of class satire: "Je me crus trop heureux d'en être oublié; persuadé qu'un Grand nous fait assez de bien quand il ne nous fait pas de mal" (I, 2). In his key terms, "grand," "bien," and "mal," Figaro achieves a devaluation of the powerful, in whom "le bien" and "le mal" are

identified. For him the only virtue possible to the great is ab-
stention from malevolence. This conclusion is obtained by
Figaro's equating the affirmative and negative forms of the
same verb ("fait" = "ne fait pas"), an equivalence made possible by the opposed meanings of the two complements. Figaro
thus unites in the same sentence two affirmations, which, taken
together, represent a specious identity. Were "bien" and "mal"
reversed a moral platitude would result. Figaro's epigram is
a stroke of wit only.

After a brief detour the same subject is continued:

> Le Comte. —Tu ne dis pas tout. Je me souviens qu'à mon service tu
> étais un assez mauvais sujet.
> Figaro. —Eh! mon Dieu, Monseigneur, c'est qu'on veut que le pauvre
> soit sans défaut. (I, 2)

Here again Figaro seemingly accepts the reproach, only to
reject it as logically ill-founded, since no one is faultless.
Thus he returns the accusation to its source, the rich. But
the count persists—"paresseux, derangé"—since he too knows
that laziness is Figaro's mistress. And Figaro ripostes with
the now famous lines:

> Aux vertus qu'on exige dans un Domestique, Votre Excellence connaît-
> elle beaucoup de Maîtres qui fussent dignes d'être Valets? (I, 2)

The friendly impudence which characterizes Figaro in both
plays is nowhere better revealed than in this remark. The
principal comic effect results from the contrast between respectful form[3] and annoying content. Ironic wit prompts Figaro
to associate "valet" (himself) with "vertu" while implying the
opposite for "maître" (the count). To Charles Lalo the comic
devaluation would here be most important, while Elie Aubouin
would say that the sense of the ludicrous is stimulated most by
the sudden identification of opposites.[4] It should be noted that if
"maîtres" were substituted for "domestiques" and "valets,"
and *vice versa*, the sentence would still be amusing, though
the social devaluation would disappear and the comic effect
lose its force. This suggests the pertinence of Lalo's view.
This same theme, "maître" *vs.* "valet", is many times repeated by the same couple, with much the same result.

Except for Figaro's tirade on the republic of letters, we pass

over the rest of Act I, scene 2, as too specialized for significant comic content. But the tirade, which forecasts his long
speech in Act V of *Le Mariage de Figaro*, is of great interest:

C'est mon bon ange, Excellence, puisque je suis assez heureux pour
retrouver mon ancien Maître. Voyant à Madrid que la république des
Lettres était celle des loups, toujours armés les uns contre les autres,
et que, livrés au mépris où ce risible acharnement les conduit, tous
les Insectes, les Moustiques, les Cousins, les Critiques, les Marin-
gouins, les Envieux, les Feuillistes, les Libraires, les Censeurs,
et tout ce qui s'attache à la peau des malheureux Gens de Lettres,
achevait de déchiqueter et sucer le peu de substance qui leur restait;
fatigué d'écrire, ennuyé de moi, dégoûté des autres, abîmé de dettes
et léger d'argent; à la fin, convaincu que l'utile revenu du rasoir est
préférable aux vains honneurs de la plume, j'ai quitté Madrid', et, mon
bagage en sautoir, parcourant philosophiquement les deux Castilles,
la Manche, l'Estramadure, la Sierra-Morena, l'Andalousie; accueilli
dans une ville, emprisonné dans l'autre, et partout supérieur aux
événements; loué par ceux-ci, blâmé par ceux-là; aidant au bon temps,
supportant le mauvais; me moquant des sots, bravant les méchants;
riant de ma misère et faisant la barbe à tout le monde; vous me voyez
enfin établi à Séville et prêt à servir de nouveau Votre Excellence en
tout ce qu'il lui plaira de m'ordonner. (I, 2)

This explanation, Figaro's response to a somewhat factitious question, is a *tour de force*, not organic to the action.
He sees to it, of course, that his own merit does not suffer;
rather he exploits the scorn of "criticasters" current in Beaumarchais' time and produces a self-justifying riot of satire.
When the play was first acted many understood Paris for
Madrid and Beaumarchais himself for Figaro, no doubt to
their great delight. The passage thus carries a double meaning,
of content and of personal association. Soon, however, the
incidental author intrusion diminishes, and Figaro emerges
in his own incongruous unity, wit and barber, superior to his
misfortunes in the city and the provinces.

The satiric portion of the speech is a constellation of degrading images developed in the manner of the Précieux. The
transformation of the republic of letters into a pack of wolves
would be banal without the further depreciation whereby they
become a swarm of self-destroying vermin. Note that the assimilation, instead of going from man to insect, takes the opposite way. As insects become men the direction of the first

sentence is reversed, and, more important, as the actions of insects are transferred to men, the depreciation becomes doubly effective. The specious "mask" which justifies this double identification is seemingly the idea of parasites, but the identity rests also on the resounding analogies between the human group and the verminous. Though Figaro does not directly say so, it is understood that, because of his merits, he was a chosen victim of the noxious swarm.

As Figaro begins describing his own fortunes his manner changes from savage to melancholy and soon to the humorous and paradoxical tone which is normal for him. This he maintains through a spate of antitheses: "abîmé de dettes et léger d'argent, " "rasoir/plume, " "accueilli/emprisonné, " "loué/ blâmé, " and others. These oppositions are resolved in an assertion of Figaro's triumph, material and spiritual, over the vermin of Madrid and over outrageous fortune in general. So complete, verbally, is his revenge upon the hostile world, that one wonders if the count too is not a victim of it. In any event, he soon will be.

Immediately, of course, the count does no more than offer his servant an opportunity for a brilliant summary:

Le Comte. —Qui t'a donné une philosophie aussi gaie?
Figaro. —L'habitude du malheur. Je me presse de rire de tout, de peur
     d'être obligé d'en pleurer. . . . (I, 2)

This is almost a definition of humor. It suggests Figaro's earlier use of "misère" to explain his fatness. Actually he asserts that in the world "malheur" is the only objective reality. His spirited response, however, is such that "malheur" and "gaieté" are speciously reconciled through wit, and Figaro's character is the creation of his own will rather than of circumstances.

Thus, despite Gouhier's opinion, [5] Figaro, already emerging as the main character, possesses a personal, but humorous, history without any loss of comic potential. This scene is no hors d'oeuvre; it is necessary to establish Figaro's amused view of human action, past, present, and future, for this is the view which the reader is to share.

Scene 3 returns to present and future action, an important aspect of which is defined by the very title of the song which

Rosine drops, *La Précaution inutile*. Precaution is the basis of Bartholo's character and his efforts. Between him and Rosine, young and spirited, there can be nothing but hostility. In the romantic sensibility youth calls to youth, and age has no hearing. Moreover, Bartholo is immediately rendered objectionable, the proper victim of intrigue and defeat He is the *senex* of traditional comedy,[6] jealous, tyrannical, scornful of vitality. Alone among the major characters, he values stagnation and directs his energy futilely to a kind of self-gratification which the reader can find only repellent. The dance of life will go on despite him. Were the doctor otherwise, his tirade on the "sottises" of the present age would be comic through the reduction of such diversity to a factitious unity. As it is, the ridicule which he intends recoils upon himself. In action too he is immediately ridiculous. For all his precautions Rosine successfully communicates with her admirer, and the folly with which Bartholo chides himself ("Bartholo, vous n'êtes qu'un sot") takes on an ironic meaning. Thus the unprotected Rosine defeats authority. This is a classical device of comedy, and it will be many times repeated in the play.

When the count and Figaro have found the message which Rosine has sent fluttering down, Figaro's wit again comes into play:

Figaro. —Monseigneur, je ne suis plus en peine des motifs de votre mascarade; vous faites ici l'amour en perspective.
Le Comte. —Te voilà instruit, mais si tu jases. . . .
Figaro. —Moi jaser! Je n'emploierai point pour vous rassurer les grandes phrases d'honneur et de dévouement dont on abuse à la journée; je n'ai qu'un mot: mon intérêt vous répond de moi; pesez tout à cette balance, etc. . . . (I, 4)

Once again Figaro leads with an affirmation which turns to negation. To make love in prospect is not yet to have made love, and the count can scarcely be flattered by the observation. Since, however, there is something to be gained Figaro hastens to acquiesce, indeed to be of assistance. He chooses words like "intérêt," "pesez," and "balance," all suggesting a monetary motive. These overcome the count's specious "honneur" and "dévouement," and his motives too are reduced to the materialistic and thus degraded. Of course, Figaro does not for a moment suspect his master of matrimonial intentions.

But the count quickly makes clear that he does indeed intend marriage, and thus arises an opportunity for the reader to learn of Bartholo's lying precaution, that of pretending that Rosine is his wife. This in turn leads to Figaro's defamatory sketch of the doctor.

The chief rhetorical devices here are, of course, antithesis and verbal consonance. Bartholo's qualities become comic because some exclude each other—for example, *beau* and *gros*— while others are connected only through sonority. It is likewise only sound which gives unity to the verbs. Yet the resulting absurdity is appropriate to the unstable Bartholo. The physical portrait is preponderantly ugly and contradictory, closely anticipating the moral portrait. *Avare* and *amoureux* are normally exclusive, and the intrigue of the play is partly built on this opposition. Similarly, *la haine* is opposed to *l'amour* and renders it meaningless. Hence the propriety of Figaro's laconic conclusion concerning *ses moyens de plaire,* a single word which summarizes and stops his outburst of virtuosity. Figaro's adjective applies also to Bartholo's probity, though here we note also his favorite trick of saying "yes" and "no" in the same breath.[7]

A successful intrigue comes nearer to realization when Figaro reveals that he owes his insight into Bartholo to the fact that he is one of the few who has access to Bartholo's closely guarded house. It is little wonder then that Figaro is suspicious of the count's access of friendship:

Le Comte *(l'embrasse).* —Ah! Figaro, mon ami, tu seras mon ange, mon libérateur, mon Dieu tutélaire.
Figaro. —Peste! comme l'utilité vous a bientôt rapproché les distances! parlez-moi des gens passionnés! (I, 4)

Figaro here devaluates both himself and his master—himself by his suggestion that, despite the extravagant language, self-advantage is the count's sole motivation. This is to be expected, perhaps, in a master-servant relationship. The count, however, suffers the more serious indignity of being reminded how recently he pronounced Figaro a rascal. In the count's reversal are established, to Figaro's advantage, two amusing equations: *coquin=ami* and *utilité=libérateur.*

Despite these sharp exchanges Figaro and the count conclude

their alliance. Figaro sketches a simple strategy of infiltration which will involve drugging the servants and rapid action to forestall the doctor's suspicion. Through a kind of good luck that passes unchallenged in comedy an opportunity is immediately at hand, and Figaro persuades his master to invade the house as a drunken soldier. It is their further good luck to hear, from their hiding place, Bartholo planning his secret marriage for the next day.

With these developments the main characters are not only well introduced but symmetrically arranged about Rosine. Bartholo, soon to be seconded by Bazile, has legal authority over her, but his abuse of power has already weakened his hold and will weaken it further. The count has the advantage of youth, rank, riches; his power over her is in the ascendant. Etienne Souriau points out that this symmetrical distribution of forces is particularly adapted to comedy and confirms the fixity of the characters.[8] They will be at the end what they were in the beginning, the conflict having changed them little, just as it could not alter the reality in which they were involved.[9] Even the two major changes—the success of the lovers and the frustration of Bartholo—are from the beginning foregone conclusions consistent with comic justice.

It is evident, moreover, that Figaro is the detached manipulator. He originates the count's role, arranges the stage, removes the obstacles or so minimizes them that there can be no heroic struggle. In other words Figaro identifies himself with the intrigue,[10] and it is principally through him that the play becomes a joyous contest. (See Charles Lalo, *Esthétique du rire*, p. 13.)

From the beginning the assailing forces have marked advantages. They know their adversary and his plans, and are themselves unsuspected. Even more important, they have in Rosine an ally within the fortress. Their first real success comes in Act I, scene 6, when Lindor's suit is favorably received. Even the count's ineptitude in verse ("Je ne sais pas faire de vers, moi") is no obstacle, for, as Figaro shrewdly remarks, "en amour le coeur n'est pas difficile sur les productions de l'esprit." An amusing interplay continues between Lindor's infatuation and Figaro's disenchantment. Both admire

Rosine, but for different reasons:

> Le Comte. – . . . Que de grâces! Que d'esprit!
> Figaro. –Que de ruse! Que d'amour!
> Le Comte. –Crois-tu qu'elle se donne à moi, Figaro?
> Figaro. –Elle passera plutôt à travers cette jalousie que d'y manquer.
> Le Comte. –C'en est fait, je suis à ma Rosine . . . pour la vie.
> Figaro. –Vous oubliez, Monseigneur, qu'elle ne vous entend plus. [11]
>   (I, 6)

Here are several levels of comic expression. Figaro's first response, in parallel construction, to the count's raptures is ironic and deflating, and he transforms Rosine's admirable qualities into a dubious one *(ruse)*. But his next exclamation reconciles the contrasting elements in *amour*, which thus takes on a significant ambiguity. The second stage shows an analogous transposition, but this time the sentiment reveals itself in an extravagant gesture, a widely recognized feature of the comic described by Bergson. Finally—and here Figaro most characteristically reveals himself—the count's constancy is reduced to emptiness by Figaro's reminding him that the proper object of his ecstasy can no longer hear him. If Figaro accepts his master's protestations, it is only because his own interests are so best served: "Allons, Figaro, vole à la fortune." His own profit and the intrigue itself are Figaro's chief concerns. And so, before leaving the stage he reiterates the plan of attack, incidentally making clear once more that, servant though he is, he controls the intrigue, while the count is subject to his orders. His last direction, like Iago's, is "de l'or dans vos poches." The repetitions stress the importance which he attaches to money, "le nerf de l'intrigue." Figaro has already specified that Bazile is *à genoux devant un écu*. Thus is established a moral similarity between the adversaries' main supporters, and this becomes more pronounced as the action progresses.

Act II

The monologue which opens Act II reveals that Figaro has succeeded in the first part of his program. Marceline is ill, and in Rosine's remark, "tous les gens sont occupés," Figaro's very words from Act I, scene 4 are echoed. In the scene which follows, Figaro is intent upon his second tactic, awakening

Rosine's love. Having heard her answer sung to Lindor (I, 6),
Figaro anticipates no difficulty. Accordingly, the comedy which
emerges in Act II, scene 2, the only scene in which Figaro and
Rosine function as a couple on stage, has a distinctive quality.
Figaro's task is to make Rosine confess, despite her maidenly
denials, that she is in love with Lindor. The comic mood then
derives from the contradiction within Rosine of her real sentiments and her conventionalized assertions, with truth finally
piercing the wall of propriety. In dialogue, though not in psychological exploration, the scene is reminiscent of Marivaux.

For Rosine, who has just finished her clandestine letter but
does not know how to convey it, Figaro's arrival is the luck
which she has been hoping for. The scene which follows moves
rapidly, and the resulting schematic quality heightens the comedy, which in other respects is somewhat restrained. Figaro
achieves his end by a series of clearly marked maneuvers and
responses. After an encouraging, though indirect, compliment
("il [l'ennui] n'engraisse que les sots"), he praises Lindor,
pretendedly a member of his own family, but warns Rosine of
a grave defect: *il est amoureux*. Choosing to understand *amou-*
reux specifically rather than generally, Rosine feigns a convincing mystification. With her question ". . . et nomme-t-il
la personne qu'il aime?" Figaro begins his second maneuver
with a refusal to impart such a confidence to her of all people.
Despite the surface double meaning this fools no one, but
Rosine's *pro forma* avowal of disinterested interest allows
him his rapturous sketch, parodying the lover's own language,
of the well-known fair. Together they take slow steps *(ville,*
quartier, rue, à deux pas) toward identity. Still Rosine teases
Figaro to name a name, but he will give her no more than *la*
pupille de votre Tuteur.

This is Rosine's cue to be covered with a pretty confusion,
and Figaro's to launch his third maneuver. She must confess
her feelings more conclusively. First he turns aside her "vous
me faites trembler." This is easy. He interprets "trembler"
in the sense of "to fear," and then taking *mal* to mean physical
ill rather than moral, he speciously concludes that there is no
reason to be afraid and hence no evil to fear. Presumably satisfied, she goes to another contradiction: "S'il m'aime, il doit
me le prouver en restant absolument tranquille." This time

Figaro's refutation is in his rhetorical question suggesting the
incompatibility of *amour* and *repos*. The rest of his reply is
a verbal trick whereby an optional contrast is made exigent
by "ce terrible choix." And both prefer *amour* to *repos*. Rosine
now gives Figaro his chance in saying, "il est certain qu'une
jeune personne ne peut empêcher un honnête homme de l'estimer." Rosine at least overtly uses *estimer* in the sense of respect, but Figaro, repeating it, turns it toward *aimer* though
without any loss of reputable connotation. Rosine follows, as-
sociating herself with Lindor in "nous perdrait." Thus he reconciles the divergent meanings of *estimer* and gives Rosine
a rationalization for doing as she wishes, that is, giving Figaro
the letter to deliver. This is, of course, a distinct avowal, at
variance with simple esteem and accordingly cannot fail to be
comical. Somewhat the same quicksilver logic is repeated with
amitié, as Figaro's ironical reply, "l'amour a bien une autre
allure," again directs the meaning to *amour*, and again she
tacitly agrees. Finally Figaro reassures her and relieves her
of responsibility with his image of the fire and the brazier,
and she is assured that the true nature of her affection will be
understood.

Throughout the scene Figaro maintains his favorite tech-
nique-replying without appearing to do so, consenting to objec-
tions, even justifying them, but somehow transforming them
into arguments to his own advantage. Rosine is an excellent
pupil. Using Figaro's technique with remarkable precocity,
she manages to acknowledge her love without verbally avowing
it. This is a scene of delicate fencing between allies, strongly
reminiscent of Marivaux in attitudes and often in language.

The scene which almost immediately succeeds presents a
sharp contrast in comic method. Now the laughter is provoked
by Bartholo's raging and by the contrast between his assertive-
ness and his impotence. Moreover, he is profoundly ignorant.
Rosine, the hidden Figaro, the audience—all are far better informed than he. Even the fact that his conduct toward Rosine
is overbearing, anticipating Bartholo's heightened odium of
scene 15, contributes to comic effect by stimulating in the
audience the appetite for punishment frequent in purely satirical comedy. When he reverts to the paper which Rosine
dropped (I, 3) Bartholo brings further ridicule on himself.

Suspicious of everything, he is suspicious of women who drop
papers, pretendedly by accident: ". . . c'est toujours quelqu'un
posté là exprès qui ramasse les papiers qu'une femme a l'air
de laisser tomber par mégarde. "[12] As a generalization, this
is foolish, but in the concrete instance Bartholo happens to be
right, though without knowing it. It is as if Bartholo is almost
to fall into a trap which he clearly sees.

The same comic device soon recurs as Bartholo testily questions Rosine about Figaro:

Bartholo.— . . . Ce Barbier n'est pas entré chez vous, au moins?
Rosine.—Vous donne-t-il aussi de l'inquiétude?
Bartholo.—Tout comme un autre.
Rosine.—Que vos répliques sont honnêtes!
Bartholo.—Ah! fiez-vous à tout le monde, et vous aurez bientôt à la
    maison une bonne femme pour vous tromper, de bons amis pour
    vous la souffler et de bons valets pour les y aider.
. . . .
Rosine.—Mais, Monsieur, s'il suffit d'être homme pour nous plaire,
    pourquoi donc me déplaisez-vous si fort?
Bartholo (stupéfait).—Pourquoi? . . . Pourquoi? . . . Vous ne ré-
    pondez pas à ma question sur ce Barbier.
Rosine.—Eh bien oui, cet homme est entré chez moi, je l'ai vu, je
    lui ai parlé. Je ne vous cache pas même que je l'ai trouvé fort
    aimable; et puissiez-vous en mourir de dépit! (Elle sort.) (II, 4)

Again, Bartholo is both right and wrong, but his conduct is totally ridiculous for several reasons. He cannot resist generalizing his irritation into another tirade against the universe, and
Rosine springs the trap on him. Gracelessly, he returns to the
question of fact only to be maneuvered into accepting Rosine's
version of his *inquiétude*. Her final speech is entirely truthful
and entirely misleading. Like Figaro, Rosine has answered
without answering, and Bartholo has learned what he wished
to without being in a position, thanks to his obsession with precautions, to profit from it.

As targets for Bartholo's rage the two valets, ironically
named, are useless. They only add to his humiliation by showing the effectiveness of Figaro's scheme. Yawning, sneezing,
and hobbling, they are like sleepwalkers, unable to act human-
ly. Thus reduced to caricature, they are perfect examples of
the comedy of the mechanical which Bergson emphasizes. [13]
They provoke Bartholo into being further ridiculous and odious.

From his railing emerge delusions of grandeur. There is no justice, no truth even, except in his own will:"... Si je ne veux pas qu'elle soit vraie, je prétends bien qu'elle ne soit pas vraie. " Of course, his questioning of his valets is useless. No one can tell him anything except what he wishes to hear. And so he concludes that his original suspicion of Figaro is right: "le maraud voudrait me payer mes cent écus sans bourse délier. " Figaro himself could not have constructed a more useful deception.

Bazile's first appearance comes without introduction or personal history. It has already been noted that to a degree he is Figaro's counterpart, though more cynical and less scrupulous. He has no difficulty in serving an evil cause, and he avows his lack of scruples and his cowardice with pedantic complacency. Bartholo's habitual raging and Bazile's self-important calm make a schematic contrast, but since the two have the same object their reconciled attitudes promote a comic relationship. With his fancy envisioning armed ambush, Bartholo does not at first understand Bazile's advice, and this is repeated in a famous speech which Beamarchais added in 1772:

> La calomnie, Monsieur? Vous ne savez guère ce que vous dédaignez; j'ai vu les plus honnêtes gens près d'en être accablés. Croyez qu'il n'y a pas de plate méchanceté, pas d'horreurs, pas de conte absurde, qu'on ne fasse adopter aux oisifs d'une grande Ville, en s'y prenant bien: et nous avons ici des gens d'une adresse! . . . D'abord un bruit léger, rasant le sol comme une hirondelle avant l'orage, *pianissimo* murmure et file, et sème en courant le trait empoisonné. Telle bouche le recueille et *piano, piano,* vous le glisse en l'oreille adroitement. Le mal est fait, il germe, il rampe, il chemine et *rinforzando* de bouche en bouche il va le diable; puis tout à coup, ne sais comment, vous voyez la Calomnie se dresser, siffler, s'enfler, grandir à vue d'oeil; elle s'élance, étend son vol, tourbillonne, enveloppe, arrache, entraîne, éclate et tonne et devient, grâce au Ciel, un cri général, un *crescendo* public, un *chorus* universel de haine et de proscription. − Qui diable y résisterait? (II, 8)

It is not easy to determine the comic value of this masterly bit, for the reader's responses are necessarily complex, and, moreover, Bazile is here conscious of producing a *tour de force*. The stages in the progress of calumny as it is loosed on the world are marked by the musical terms in their appropriate sequence. By pointing to a contrast between the harmony expected of music and the destructiveness of slander, these sug-

gest the music teacher's professional deformity, as well as his
pedantry. The terms, however, only frame, rather than reveal, the progressing thought. The operative words in this
passage are verbs. *Murmure* suggests the first rustling movement; *germe, rampe, chemine* its stealthy extension. Then
suddenly the storm breaks loose as sound in *siffler, éclate,
tonne;* as sight in *grandir* and *s'élance;* as force in *enveloppe,
arrache, entraîne.* The over-all movement of this passage and
the impression it makes are portentous and poetic more than
comic, and Bazile thus attains momentarily a kind of sinister
grandeur. The comic resides, however, in the disparity between the language and the contemptible content; baseness has
taken on, in Bazile's mouth, the tone of nature in convulsion.
The final sentence, lapsing into the vulgar, re-emphasizes the
contrast and prompts a laugh of relaxation which carries with
it the annihilation of Bazile's pompous effort.

For all this farrago of advice, it is evident that Bazile has
done nothing to hasten Bartholo's marriage. The reason again
points to the central, almost the sole, fact of Bazile's character, his devotion to money:

> . . . vous avez lésiné sur les frais, et, dans l'harmonie du bon ordre,
> un mariage inégal, un jugement inique, un passe-droit évident, sont
> des dissonances qu'on doit toujours préparer et sauver par l'accord
> parfait de l'or. (II, 8)

This is much the same policy as Figaro recommended to the
count in Act I, scene 6. There is a further comic effect in the
continuance of the musical analogy. The specious justification
rests on the double sense, musical and social, of *l'harmonie.*
Offences are dissonances, but if transformed by the accord
which money can impose on any situation, they become useful
to the general harmony. On the surface it seems that ordinary
values are themselves degraded, but the known character of
the speaker actually turns the devaluation against himself and
against Bartholo, who concurs in his advice.

The ease with which Figaro, aided again by Bartholo's excessive precaution, escapes with valuable information which
he has overheard is one more instance of the unequal conflict
persisting through the play. Likewise Figaro's facile excuse
for eavesdropping. Using the common connotations of *écouter*

and *entendre* to establish a specious identity between them, he has no trouble in persuading Rosine—and the reader—that his conduct deserves no reproach.

But this triumph is suddenly disturbed as Bartholo resumes pestering Rosine with questions about Figaro's visit. Despite some agile lying Rosine does not succeed in explaining the ink stain, the missing sheet of paper, damaging bits of evidence though wholly circumstantial. It is only through the chance of interruption that Rosine emerges safe from this skirmish, which is to be resumed in scene 15.

The count's mask of drunkenness, recommended by Figaro, has several comic advantages. It amounts to a disguise, furnishing two mutually exclusive impressions of one person. It enables the count to communicate directly with Rosine under Bartholo's very nose. It mocks the pretended astuteness of Bartholo, the only one who does not penetrate the disguise. It enables the count, finally, to jeer at Bartholo in a manner gratifying to himself, Rosine, and the reader.[14] The doctor is so blind in his self-conceit that he cannot recognize his enemy, even when evidence is flaunted before him and the count proclaims that he has something to hide. Bartholo cannot imagine an enemy, drunk or sober, so boldly revealing himself, and he is thus the perfect dupe of a mask. As before, the contest is schematically unequal.

The rout continues as Bartholo, who should not try to meet the count's free-ranging wit, objects to the *signalement*.[15] This provokes a tirade which reintroduces the image of Bartholo as an old woman. Soon follow insults to Bartholo's profession and a reminder of Figaro's witty account of his career as a horse-and-peasant doctor. Even the count is astonished at his own virtuosity, which enables him temporarily to attain something like Figaro's cleverness. For when Bartholo lauds his own profession, "un art dont le soleil s'honore d'éclairer les succès," the count can crush him with "et dont la terre s'empresse de couvrir les bévues."[16] The statements are opposed in tone and content, but they apply to the same facts and correspond in terms and syntax. Thus the opposed meanings are masked so that the words placed in like positions *(s'honore/ s'empresse, éclairer/couvrir, succès/bévues)* are unified, reconciled despite their diversity. The ultimate intent is plainly

the reduction of *succès* to the level of *bévues*. These lines
might almost have been written to illustrate Lalo's "équation
du rire esthétique."

The onslaught continues until Bartholo has, with his own
consent and assistance, been deflated, as a man and as a
doctor, and rendered stupid. When the count puts his last
rhetorical question, "est-ce que vous ne le voyez pas," everyone except Bartholo, the most interested in the principals, can
reply in the affirmative.

When Rosine re-enters she and the count are able to maintain
a communication from which only Bartholo is excluded. Much
of this is effected by verbal legerdemain. The count quickly
deflects Rosine's "un homme qui déraisonne" to Bartholo, and
sets up his rapport with her in "nous sommes raisonnables,
nous." This is reinforced by the rhyming words *poli* and *jolie*.
Even so, the count's most difficult feat remains: safely passing
the letter to Rosine in Bartholo's presence. Once he has failed.
This time he attempts to prepare Rosine:

Le Comte.— . . . s'il y a de l'obscurité dans mes phrases . . . [17]
Rosine.—J'en saisirai l'esprit.
Le Comte.—Non, attachez-vous à la lettre, à la lettre. (II, 14)

There is a comic value in the reversal of the conventional
importance of *lettre* and *esprit*, particularly since the two
are trying to circumvent "law" as represented by Bartholo.
But since an actual letter exists, no absurdity enters. Bartholo, however, sees nothing of this letter. Rather his attention
is called to the order for billeting "Lindor, dit l'Ecolier, Ca-
valier du Régiment." Here Bartholo's exemption from har-
boring soldiers gives him a momentary triumph, though a
dangerous one, because it obliges him to leave Rosine for a
moment unguarded. The time, however, is not enough to pass
the letter, and Bartholo's vigilance overreaches itself as he
warns the count away from his "wife." To gain time and to express his rancor, the count vents more ridicule: "Je vous ai
pris pour son bisaïeul paternel, maternel, sempiternel; il y a
au moins trois générations entre elle et vous."[18] Here Beaumarchais reverts to a device used early in the scene, comic
unification or mask through sound. As far as meaning goes, the

phrase *trois générations* makes it obvious that for the count the
sonorous adjectives are only superlatives of time.

To achieve his purpose the count finally has to resort to
a kind of scuffling which transforms the scene briefly into
farce.[19] Once more Bartholo is covered with ridicule, handled
roughly, frustrated. In the past he has been repeatedly blind;
here he is only impotent. The scene ends with some gratuitous
insulting which is yet witty enough to re-establish a tone of
comedy. The three final speeches are linked by the repetition
of *mort;* the meanings, however, are divergent. Finally the
opposition between *mort* and *vie* as they appear in the first
speech is resolved in the last in a final sneer, put as before
with feigned politeness, at Bartholo's profession: the death of
others is life for him.

It is obvious that Bartholo was not so much deceived by
the count as he was overwhelmed. Too confident now of his
authority, he insists on seeing the letter, not at all believing Rosine's dodge about a letter from her cousin. But Bartholo is no match for her. She belabors him with unpleas-
ant truths about himself—and this in a context of her own lies
—and then with an improbable ruse persuades him that he has
been not only mistaken but odious. His momentary triumph
becomes Rosine's, and nothing he can do or say restores his
loss.

Rosine trusts to a kind of boldness which makes her often
seem careless of her own security. This has been evident in
the lies of Act I, scene 3. Here again when she feigns anger,
faints, juggles the two letters to assure the discovery she
wishes, she brazenly assumes a kind of disguise which deceives no one but Bartholo. These actions promote also a comedy of gestures and suggest the resemblance of her role and
the count's.

As soon as Bartholo is submissive, however, she reverts
to the same logical game she played in Act II, scene 4:

Bartholo.—. . . . Si tu pouvais m'aimer! Ah, comme tu serais heu-
reuse!
Rosine.—Si vous pouviez me plaire, ah! comme je vous aimerais!
Bartholo.—Je te plairai, je te plairai; quand je te dis que je te plairai.
    (II, 15)

The symmetrical constructions screen a violent contrast. *Pouvoir* and *plaire* change in meaning as they pass from one character to the other. Indeed, Rosine uses them to affirm her indifference to Bartholo, and thus presents another variation of the theme of his nullity, as a man, in her esteem. It is again Bartholo who, whether through timidity, passing delicacy, or clumsiness, gives his pupil the opportunity to use destructive logic against him. His *tu serais heureuse* really means *je serais heureux*. Rosine corrects him. Happiness depends only on himself; all he need do is please her. And Bartholo, as a crowning absurdity, promises this impossibility, a typical action of a ridiculous character. The ambiguity in *plaire* is not dissipated, and the dialogue ends in Bartholo's total misunderstanding.

Anger, authority, submission—none of Bartholo's tactics gains him anything but frustration. In all respects his worth as a man and a lover is destroyed. Moreover, by opposing himself to common sense he has lost all the spectator's sympathy. His irony cannot strike anyone and recoils on himself. Rosine has shown herself almost as adroit as Figaro at reducing an adversary to absurdity, at making his injurious (and accurate) suppositions turn back against him, and at telling him the truth without exposing herself.

Act III

Bartholo's brief monologue makes it clear that Rosine has resumed her quarrel with him in accordance with her decision of the previous scene. Her pretext is resentment of Bazile's involvement in the prospective marriage. So when the count reappears, now disguised as a music teacher and pupil of Bazile, Bartholo has a strong reason for accepting him. For a second time Bartholo falls into the same trap.[20] He is deceived again by the disguise and again by the count's trick of revealing a part of the truth, confident that it will not be believed. Even so, there are some flaws in the count's maneuvering. Bartholo frightens him into a contradiction about Bazile's "illness." He has to play his dangerous game of showing Rosine's letter, threatened by her overhearing the conversation; hence, like

Bartholo, he must beg his adversary to speak softly. Moreover, he had intended only to show the letter; by losing it to
Bartholo he causes a diversion which delays his triumph.

Altogether, however, the scene is the count's, for he successfully persuades Bartholo that "Alonzo" is Bazile's faithful servant, ready for any roguery. The height of irony occurs
when Bartholo himself introduces the enemy into the fortress,
pleased because he appears to be more *un amant déguisé* than
un ami officieux. Bartholo speaks the exact truth, though he
does not know it.[21]

To produce these comic effects, the result of Bartholo's
twice falling into the same trap, Beaumarchais was obliged
occasionally to reduce Bartholo's intelligence to stupidity and
to show him speechless where an apt reply would save him.
The variants prove that Beaumarchais was aware of the danger
of psychological improbability and sought to minimize it. The
best avoidance came in his efforts to show Bartholo dominated
not so much by simple ineptitude as by false logic, a method
which is freely used also in *Le Mariage de Figaro*. Its use
here results in the count's having the principal active role
in provoking comedy, and he does so by maneuvers imitated
from his master Figaro.

Tension increases briefly early in scene 4 as Rosine first
refuses the music lesson and then, suddenly recognizing the
count, almost betrays him. A moment later it is Bartholo who
is threatening to send "Alonzo" on his way.[22] A more discern-
ing suspicion might have seen through Rosine's ready but specious excuse for being alarmed. Soon Rosine and "Alonzo" are
in control of the scene. Bartholo feels only distaste at the
choice of a song from *La Précaution inutile,* unaware that both
lovers are adept at putting in song what would be dangerous to
speak. Bartholo's sudden lapse from vigilance into slumber is
more a stage contrast than a plausible action, and upon awakening he is sufficiently relaxed to match the song he did not
hear with a parody. It is equally surprising that, having whis-
pered of "mille choses essentielles à vous dire, " the count
should take advantage of Bartholo's nap for nothing more useful
than kissing Rosine's hand. Indeed, so far in the scene no
character has been conspicuous for intelligence. Perhaps this

illustrates inversely Souriau's dictum that overly perspicacious characters are a danger to comedy *(Les Deux cent milles situations dramatiques,* p. 224).

With Figaro's "entry, " after his parody of Bartholo's parody, a certain sharpness returns to the action and dialogue. This is Figaro's first encounter with the doctor, and Bartholo concentrates in the heavy irony of his greeting all the annoyance he has good reason to feel. Here and for several speeches to come Figaro chooses to ignore all but the literal meaning of Bartholo's words, thus damping his fury until the doctor explodes in a sarcastic question:

. . . Que direz-vous, Monsieur le zélé, à ce malheureux qui baîlle et dort tout éveillé? Et l'autre qui, depuis trois heures, éternue à se faire sauter le crâne et jaillir la cervelle! que leur direz-vous?
   (III, 5)

This is a mistake. Bartholo intended a crushing rhetorical question, but Figaro gives *dire* an entirely banal sense, then offers a false lead which Bartholo is all too prone to follow. Yet he is tempted to a reproach concerning the poultice on his mule's eyes. This time even Bartholo can see, aided perhaps by a gesture, that Figaro's *d'y voir* might apply to himself, and he hastily returns to a complaint about the bill. Now Figaro allows Bartholo the joy of having discovered his motives. Indeed, he opens himself to the accusation, and only Bartholo is unaware that he has himself furnished the mask which deceives him:

Ma foi, Monsieur, les hommes n'ayant guère à choisir qu'entre la sottise et la folie, où je ne vois pas de profit, je veux au moins du plaisir; et vive la joie! Qui sait si le monde durera encore trois semaines? (III, 5)

If Figaro's premise is granted, life's significance is impudently reduced to a primary concern for material advantage. That failing, one can only seek another kind of *profit,* which is *plaisir,* that is, confounding someone like Bartholo.

Bartholo presumably thinks himself adroit in refusing to pursue this latest diversion, but actually he continues playing the game Figaro wishes:

Bartholo.—Vous feriez bien mieux, Monsieur le raisonneur, de me
   payer mes cent écus et les intérêts sans lanterner, je vous en
   avertis.
Figaro.—Doutez-vous de ma probité, Monsieur? Vos cent écus! j'aimerais mieux vous les devoir toute ma vie que de les nier un seul
   instant. (III, 5)

Bartholo might well be tempted to take this as a genuine pro-
testation of honesty. Even the reader may feel so for a moment,
and thus, experiencing Aubouin's *conciliation des inconciliables*, may believe that Figaro is about to pay his debt at once.
But laughter comes with the delayed dawning of truth: actually
Figaro is telling Bartholo that he never will be paid. Once
more he has approached the negative through the affirmative.
   As the scene continues Beaumarchais brings dialogue and
action together again with Figaro's unexpected embarrassment
over the bonbons. Even his agility cannot make the lie convincing, and Bartholo has a seemingly perfect opportunity for
reproach:

Bartholo.—. . . Vous faites là un joli métier, Monsieur!
Figaro.—Qu'est-ce qu'il a donc, Monsieur?
Bartholo.—Et qui vous fera une belle réputation, Monsieur!
Figaro.—Je la soutiendrai,. Monsieur!
Bartholo.—Dites que vous la supporterez, Monsieur!
Figaro.—Comme il vous plaira, Monsieur!
Bartholo.—Vous le prenez bien haut, Monsieur! Sachez que quand je
   dispute avec un fat, je ne lui cède jamais.
Figaro *(lui tourne le dos)*.—Nous différons en cela, Monsieur! moi,
   je lui cède toujours! (III, 5)[23]

Here the tactics of an earlier exchange are repeated. Bartholo
presses with irony; Figaro, all humility, disguises himself in
literal understanding. Soon Bartholo cannot maintain the self-
control which irony demands and, determined to triumph, de-
livers a direct insult. Again he sets his own trap, and Figaro
solemnly springs it. The comic effect in this dialogue is steadily underscored by the contrast between the ceremonial address
and the insulting intention of the adversaries. The opposition
reaches its highest tension when *Monsieur* is identified with
fat, and at that point loses its masking value. With Bartholo
stopped short, Figaro continues the theme of his *métier*, in

a sequence much more fully developed in an earlier version,[24] and pursues his purpose of further deflating the unfortunate doctor.

This again leads dialogue away from action. They rejoin as Bartholo, exasperated to the point of sending Figaro on his way, discovers that this, and only this, is his day to be shaved. Accordingly, he is faced with a choice ruinous to his precautions: shall he quit the scene or give his key to Figaro to get his shaving gear? There is no good solution, and somewhat impulsively he rushes out himself, urging the disguised count to keep an eye on his ward and that dangerous barber, thus preparing the disaster he wishes to avoid.

The three short scenes which follow owe their comedy to rapid action, to the off-stage noise of breaking crockery, and to a general air of distraction through which unobtrusively the lovers' conspiracy is advanced. As Figaro returns from his depredations, the dialogue and action again are closely related:

Bartholo. —Je ne m'étais pas trompé; tout est brisé, fracassé.

Figaro. —Voyez le grand malheur pour tant de train! on ne voit goutte sur l'escalier. *(Il montre la clef au Comte.)* Moi, en montant, j'ai accroché une clef . . .

Bartholo. —On prend garde à ce qu'on fait. Accrocher une clef! L'habile homme!

Figaro. —Ma foi, Monsieur, cherchez-en un plus subtil. (III, 10)

This exchange is full of significant double meanings. Figaro's *on ne voit goutte* indicates that breaking the entire shaving set is no great matter and, more important for Rosine and the count, that Bartholo has no suspicions. *J'ai accroché une clef* is even bolder. Bartholo understands only that the key was caught in something and caused the accident, but the rest that Figaro has captured the necessary key. Bartholo's *habile homme* is intended to be crudely ironical, but every one else knows that it contains an unconscious compliment to Figaro's agility.

Scenes 5-10 have been analyzed to show a characteristic which is prominent in both plays, i. e., the progress of the action by a kind of tacking movement. Though he maintains the general direction, Beaumarchais feels free to introduce deviations at will, to secure a richer comic effect, even at the expense of ideal economy. To be sure, Figaro attempts a series of diversions (the mule, his probity, his calling) which are functional in that he uses them to escape admissions damaging to the intrigue. But even these have the added value of provoking laughter at Bartholo's ineptitude. It is evident that for Beaumarchais—and his audience—wit had an intrinsic value sufficient to justify disturbing, though not destroying, organic unity.

Scene 11 is perhaps the most comical of the whole play; technically it is a *tour de force* relying on reversal of situation, multiple disguised identities of the count, and an opposition between character and situation for Bartholo. [25] As disaster suddenly faces the conspirators with the appearance of Bazile, there is a moment of consternation. Then all, even Bartholo, join to overwhelm and negate the intruder. From all sides he is belabored with demands to keep quiet. These constitute almost a material impediment to his speaking, for they come so rapidly that he must face all sides at once. Thus he is turned round and round like an object with no will of its own. The key words in this phase of making Bazile ridiculous are *taisez-vous*. Everyone, it seems, knows his secret; yet everyone, with good reason, insists on his silence. The next phase is marked by repetition of *homme de loi*. Here variations in tone seem to give the phrase three different meanings, none of them comprehensible to Bazile. Now the opening situation is reversed; the bearer of news is having news thrust upon him. He is ignorant, bewildered, and inferior. With the third phase, marked by repetition of *allez-vous coucher*, Bazile is in effect expelled from the action as worse than useless. This time even Bazile participates, though still uncomprehending:

En effet, Messieurs, je crois que je ne ferai pas mal de me retirer; je sens qu je ne suis pas ici dans mon assiette ordinaire. (III, 11)

But Bazile consents to his own negation with some wit. The medical connotation of *assiette ordinaire* is cancelled by *ici*. In other words, Bazile points out that he is falling in with the game without being fooled by it, and thus his ridiculousness is attenuated. Even so, he has consented to several kinds of annihilation: his knowledge is transformed into ignorance, his health has become illness. He has, in fact, substantially renounced himself and has accepted a deficient personality foisted

on him by the others. The only valid reason is the purse offered
by the count; this is Bazile's price. In surrendering thus he ab-
jures the value he places on serving Bartholo. But he acts in
accordance with what is for him a higher value, the money
which is so much his god that it is almost his identity. Bribed,
he obtains entire satisfaction and remains "invulnerable." In
this latter sense he is a copy, though depraved, of Figaro.

With the departure of Bartholo's one ally the triumph of the
lovers seems complete. But in scene 12 Bartholo, despite
Figaro's frantic efforts, overhears the count's ill-advised
talk of disguise and denounces him—"perfide Alonzo." There
is no chance to tell Rosine that Bartholo has her letter. So for
a moment Bartholo tastes triumph.[26] But only for a moment,
for as the count speaks the words "votre femme" Rosine explodes with a fury not before seen, and all join to put him in a
position worse than Bazile's. So as the act ends, the doctor is
left alone, helplessly raging and ridiculous, even though he
recognizes his own folly.

Act IV

With Act IV the alliance of Bartholo and Bazile is rejoined,
and their plot, temporarily broken down, is set in motion
again. But the threat from this change is not grave. The reader
is aware that the lovers have their own plans well laid. Moreover, in this scene of realliance the unreliability of Bazile as
a coadjutor is emphasized:

Bartholo.—A propos de ce présent [the purse given by the Count in
    Act III, scene 11], eh! pourquoi l'avez-vous reçu?
Bazile.—Vous aviez l'air d'accord; je n'y entendais rien; et dans les
    cas difficiles à juger, une bourse d'or me paraît toujours un
    argument sans réplique. Et puis, comme dit le proverbe, ce
    qui est bon à prendre . . .
Bartholo.—J'entends; est bon . . .
Bazile.—A garder.
Bartholo *(surpris)*.—Ah! Ah!
Bazile.—Oui, j'ai arrangé comme cela plusieurs petits proverbes avec
    des variations. . . (IV, 1)

Actually, Bazile's frankly avowed self-interest is an ominous
preparation for scene 7, the occasion of Bartholo's final frustration. The music master's replies show, moreover, that he
is unassailable in his amorality. The purse is transformed

from a material object into intellectual energy; it is the un-
answerable argument, the quieter of "conscience," the deliv-
erer from any painful reflection. The proverb—that is, the
variation which suits him at the moment—likewise, if unchallenged, provides him with a perfect justification. When dis-
engaged from self-interest, Bazile is all compliance and wit.
Like Figaro he exploits a double meaning (posséder/jouir).
When he sees Bartholo resisting his advice, he resorts to
attenuated affirmation—"on en voit beaucoup cette année"—
which relieves Bartholo of all responsibility. Bartholo insists: "Il vaut mieux qu'elle [Rosine] pleure de m'avoir, que
je meure de ne l'avoir pas." And Bazile again concedes to the
point of reversing himself: "Il y va de la vie? Epousez, Docteur, épousez." The device is simple; he pretends to give real
value to the verbs in Bartholo's worn-out hyperbole, and this
ironical revaluation conceals his reversal of opinion.[27] All this
reveals Bazile to be a lesser Figaro, independent, detached,
conscious of the comedy he creates.

The remainder of the scene represents confident action which
events are soon to turn into rout. Though Bazile is sent out,
past midnight and in wretched weather, to find the lawyer,
Bartholo's haste is still tardy compared with that of the lovers.
Giving Bazile the passkey, though it seems logical, actually
works to permit the count's wedding rather than Bartholo's.
The letter and the calumny on which Bartholo puts great reli-
ance eventually recoil upon him in scene 3 when Rosine decides
to reproach Lindor directly for his treachery. There are in the
scene, moreover, two warnings which he does not heed sufficiently: Bazile's guess that the giver of the purse in Act III,
scene 11, might have been the count himself and his report of
the marriage of Figaro's "niece." All these elements combine
to make a spectacular irony of Bazile's final assurance: "Avec
ces précautions, vous êtes sûr de votre fait."

On the surface scene 3 seems the culmination of Bartholo's
triumph and the defeat of the lovers' hopes.[28] The center of the
action is Rosine's painful disillusionment with Lindor, effected
by Bartholo's careful following of Bazile's advice about the
power of calumny. For a moment the play approaches pathos,
in showing Rosine's genuine distress and the desperate resolution which she rashly bases on her lost faith. All this, how-

ever, is but the coiling of the spring which will soon be released. It reminds one that some theorists have found the principal source of laughter in the release of emotional tension.[29] One also notes an exploitation of differing expectations. It often happens in comedy that the characters' short-range view of consequences envisions calamity. Since they are passionately involved in conflict, this is almost inescapably so. The audience or reader, however, finds it easy to temper his involvement with the confidence which comes from a long-range view. Since disaster has not yet occurred, its occurrence seems unlikely, and a fortunate issue can be foreseen. Part of this response is ordinary wishful thinking, but part is a kind of logic of probability, which the characters themselves, with little chance for perspective, cannot attain.

Even in his triumph, however, Bartholo overplays his hand and announces the early arrival of the notary. His confidence that a delighted Rosine will do his bidding is misplaced. Instead she stays on the scene, to berate her treacherous lover. At any rate she is present when the undisguised count appears and with little difficulty undoes Bartholo's calumny. Again Bartholo is victim of his own logical folly. In removing the ladder he did not dream that the principals would therefore remain in the house until the arrival of Bazile and the notary or that there would be just enough time during his absence for the marriage contract to be signed.

Scene 7 returns to the comic in expression, after a scene of stage maneuvering. It opens in confusion. The encounter puzzles all present, and they greet each other in friendly, albeit ironical, tones. As the situation begins to clarify, Bazile first points out its ridiculousness, at Bartholo's expense: "Si c'est pour cela qu'il m'a donné le passe-partout." After this cynicism his scruples about signing the contract are momentarily puzzling until Figaro's goading question brings a conclusive avowal and action:

Figaro.—Où donc est la difficulté de signer?
Bazile *(pesant la bourse)*.—Il n'y en a plus; mais c'est que moi, quand j'ai donné ma parole une fois, il faut des motifs d'un grand poids. . . . *(Il signe.)* (IV, 7)

His hesitation was only a gesture of decency. Actually, Bazile not only denies his pretended *raison d'être*, serving Bartholo, but he also translates the abstract value of his morality into the concrete value of gold. The key word is *motifs*, which takes on a connotation of weight and dimension. Similarly *poids* assumes an abstract meaning as well as the concrete one. Once more opposing concepts are forcibly reconciled, and the worthier is devalued. It should be noted that Bazile is more amusing than ridiculous here. His wit saves him from being censurable even while he matches deceit with deceit. [30]

In scene 8 Bazile continues the theme with his favorite assimilation, *argument/argent:*

Bartholo.—Comment, Bazile! vous avez signé?
Bazile.—Que voulez-vous? ce diable d'homme a toujours ses poches pleines d'arguments irrésistibles. (IV, 8)

The effect is intensified when the same "argument" finally overcomes Bartholo himself:

Bazile.—. . . Ne pouvant avoir la femme, calculez, Docteur, que l'argent vous reste; et . . .
Bartholo.—Eh! laissez-moi donc en repos, Bazile! Vous ne songez qu'à l'argent. Je me soucie bien de l'argent, moi! A la bonne heure, je le garde, mais croyez-vous que ce soit le motif qui me détermine? *(Il signe.)* (IV, 8)

Despite his denials, Bartholo makes apparent his own inner contradictions, the source of his ridiculousness. He destroys the negative sense of his question by an act of consent, since he signs, thus at once affirming and denying that love and women are never worth more than money. This evinces a schism of personality quite absent from Rosine, the count, and even Figaro. [31]

In analyzing his first comedy, Beaumarchais observed that "le genre d'une pièce, comme celui de toute action, dépend moins du fond des choses que des caractères qui les mettent en oeuvre." He immediately thereafter defined his main character:

Quant à moi, ne voulant faire, sur ce plan, qu'une Pièce amusante et sans fatigue, une espèce d'*imbroille*, il m'a suffi que le Machiniste, au lieu d'être un noir scélérat, fût un drôle de garçon, un homme insouciant, qui rit également du succès et de la chute de ses entreprises, pour que l'Ouvrage, loin de tourner en Drame sérieux, devînt une Comédie fort gaie. . . .[32]

Thus Beaumarchais quite orthodoxly affirms the primacy of

character in producing comic effect, and in this we concur, noting only that by character we understand here the *attitude* of the dramatic participants, who, when confronted by exigency, refuse to get themselves involved in any deeper personal conflict or problem.

Figaro corresponds exactly to his creator's definition. He is plainly the manipulator of the intrigue, but at no time is he in any personal way affected by it, except for the one hundred *écus*. This is not to say, of course, that he does not take a lively interest in the success of his maneuvers. His detachment leaves him free to conduct the intrigue and to manipulate the other characters according to his own uncontrolled will and preconceived plan. It is this that makes him a comic personage, superior to events. This same immunity to pique or passion allows him to be amused with his own lot, a fundamental attitude which is most important in establishing the comic mood of the play for the spectator. While Figaro laughs at himself, the audience, sympathetic because he serves the favored cause, will laugh with him, but not at him. Ridicule never actually touches him. The comic atmosphere which surrounds him also serves to minimize any dramatic tension which might alienate the play from the comic. So Figaro forces his own amusement upon the willing spectator, and since the whole play is seen from his point of view he makes of the conflict a high-spirited contest.

Count Almaviva is a mixed character. Whereas Figaro is the conscious master of the comedy he creates, the count is comic mainly by virtue of his two disguises, which were suggested by Figaro, and the absurd situations they promote. In fairness we must give the count credit for the antics (I, 14) which enable him to get his letter to Rosine. Also he twice bribes Bazile (III, 2, and IV, 7)—though it was Figaro who suggested the importance of gold and the weakness of Bazile—and twice arrests potentially disastrous situations and thus prevents a transformation of mood from comic to pathetic. In these successes he is temporarily a double of Figaro. More often, however, he is a foil for Figaro and thus neither intrinsically comic nor fully developed. He never achieves by himself the verve suggested by his name.

The development of Rosine in *Le Barbier de Séville* is simi-

larly ungenerous. Like the count, she is in love and similarly
confident of her chances for eventual rescue from Bartholo.
Because she senses no real menace in her situation and is
therefore free to match ruse with ruse, she conveys a lack of
concern for her own security. Her character has undergone a
notable simplification. Except for her sudden and soon rescind-
ed expressions of tenderness for her tutor, Beaumarchais rendered her in the final version of his play less insistent upon
marriage with Bartholo at the moment of her belief that the
count has deceived her. Together, the count and Rosine share
an important passivity; they are the destined beneficiaries of
Figaro's success.

Bartholo, on the other hand, is fundamentally ridiculous.
Beaumarchais himself, in his *Lettre modérée,* defines his
character and role as follows:

. . . et [de] cela seul que le Tuteur est un peu moins sot que tous
ceux qu'on trompe au Théâtre, il a résulté beaucoup de mouvement
dans la Pièce, et surtout la nécessité d'y donner plus de ressort aux
intrigants. [33]

In other words Bartholo has to contribute to the comic through
that quality which he may consciously claim, his perspicacity,
which, however, he unfailingly misdirects to useless precautions. That we laugh with Figaro and at Bartholo goes far to
justify the distinction often made between the comic and the
ridiculous. Bartholo himself is at no time intentionally a come-
dian. He is bent on very serious business throughout the play,
and it is this wary preoccupation with something that matters
deeply to him as contrasted with its absurdly aborted results
which creates comedy. Bartholo is, moreover, a traditional
character type, an aged lover (Gouhier, *"Condition du comique"),* though with some personal history. He would easily become odious if he were actually more dangerous. He reaches
a peak of folly in the last scene of the play when he renounces
in writing his claim to Rosine and thus denies his passion in
exchange for money; he thus renounces the one feature which
might have rendered him sympathetic. This renunciation has
still another consequence: it appears finally that Bartholo's
suffering is trivial, for he is easily consoled. Indeed, one may
suspect that all along he is more interested in his own pre-
cautionary cleverness than he is in Rosine herself. Throughout

the play, then, there appear in Bartholo, the most formidable obstacle to the lovers, fundamental inconsistencies which render him laughable, not merely because of his manner, but for what he essentially is. [34] The variations attest that Beaumarchais determined the definitive amount of ridiculousness only after considerable experimenting. [35]

We find in Bazile another character who is basically ridiculous. Being in the service of the "evil" cause, he is antipathetic before any development occurs. Like Bartholo he renounces his presumed role in the play for money. But unlike Bartholo he has hardly any personal history and hence resembles the character type to whom nothing serious can happen. He represents simply the traitor who sells himself to the highest bidder without asking any explanation; thus he corresponds to the automaton and the "type" which Bergson describes. [36] Without genuine moral character, he is like Figaro—though for other reasons—with whom he shares other qualities. Bazile's obvious cleverness and wit make him a lively person, though hollow, and accentuate still further his laughable character. These two are often similar forces. It is not surprising that in an abandoned variation of the last scene Beaumarchais has them calling themselves brothers.

The variations reveal that in earlier versions, which contain many affective effusions, the play was not centered so much as it was finally either on the comic in general or in so exclusive a manner on the character of Figaro. There is reason to believe that Beaumarchais originally conceived all of his comic characters along the same general lines and that their differentiation came about through gradual simplification and elaboration.

Whatever may be the action of a play and the series of situations which compose it, these should assure the external unity of the work. It may be admitted that there is no action or situation which is comic in itself. [37] But it has also been shown that comedy requires a minimized degree of dramatic tension. [38] In other words, resistance to the efforts of the favored group must become neither insurmountable nor such as to exact heroic struggle. Were it otherwise there could be no joyous contest. If this trait of comedy depends, as Beaumarchais clearly realized, in large part upon the responses and the structure of the characters, certain peculiarities in the ordering of action permit the comic potentialities of the characters to be realized. [39]

We have pointed to the symmetrical disposition of forces. In the action this contributes to an oscillatory movement up to the point of the resolution, a movement which might have been prolonged indefinitely according to the pleasure and talents of the author. The indispensable dramatic tautness is maintained by the ever-present threat of an irruption of one or the other of the adverse forces. The irruption inevitably occurs and usually has the effect of dispersing those immediate conflicts which might alter the mood from comic to serious or even to tragic. A persistent up-and-down movement of the intrigue, then, which does not preclude surprises, is characteristic of the play. Indeed, laughter is provoked by the precipitate character of the intrigue and by the manner in which the potential sympathetic victim escapes each embarrassment.

More than once a situation is repeated with its form slightly altered, e. g., the count's two disguises. This procedure implies a gratuitous simplicity on the part of the character being duped. But the repeated situations often have different implications. The count's second pose is fraught with danger, for it is possible that Bazile will appear, and indeed he does. This accident and the moral and material substitution of himself for Bazile accomplished by the count's ruse make the repetition itself a comic device. Disguised, the same person takes on two nearly opposite significances; the count remains himself but also descends to the level of his adversaries. Beaumarchais well knew how to revitalize repeated procedures.

All the devices of action, then, in *Le Barbier de Séville* contribute to comic atmosphere: the surprise which accompanies sudden change of direction, the stylization which comes from alternating fortunes, the postponement of resolution until what appears to be an accident of the last moment, the laugh—not itself intrinsically comic—caused by release of tension.

Closely related to action are the artifices of the play. These have three principal purposes: to further the action, to make plausible the avoidance of pathos, and to maintain the unexpectedness which in this comedy is a part of the continuing interplay of advantage and disadvantage. Artifice is often the only explanation for the dealings of chance, which may have good or bad results for the sympathetic characters.

Beaumarchais was reproached by his contemporaries for too often divorcing artifice from probability. He excused himself in the *Lettre modérée*:

Un matin qu'il se promenait sous ses fenêtres à Séville, où depuis huit jours il cherchait à s'en faire remarquer, le hasard conduisit au même endroit Figaro le Barbier. "Ah! le hasard! dira mon Critique; et si le hasard n'eût pas conduit ce jour-là le Barbier dans cet endroit, que devenait la Pièce?—Elle eût commencé, mon Frère, à quelque autre époque.—Impossible, puisque le Tuteur, selon vous-même, épousait le lendemain.—Alors il n'y aurait pas eu de Pièce, ou, s'il y en avait eu, mon Frère, elle aurait été différente. Une chose est-elle invraisemblable, parce qu'elle était possible autrement? [40]

Since the play patently needed a beginning situation, this somewhat factitious explanation is acceptable enough. But one notes continued contrivance through the play. For instance, in Act II, scene 2, Bartholo's unexpected arrival prompts Figaro to hide in Rosine's music room and thus he overhears the scheming of Bartholo and Bazile. This is advantageous to Figaro's own plan of action and is also a source of comic effect, of what Souriau describes as an invasion from the exterior world *(Les Deux cent milles situations dramatiques*, p. 24). Figaro's hiding is well enough motivated, but Bartholo's arrival at the moment is pure chance. Likewise in Act II, scene 15, with the letter, which Rosine has received from her cousin, conveniently to be exchanged for the one from the count. In Act IV, scene 7, the double coincidence of passkey and ladder makes the desirable marriage possible and cleverly brings the play to an end. This artifice, however, has some foundation in character. It is consistent with Bartholo's penchant for precautions that he should give the passkey to Bazile and remove the ladder. What is more surprising is the arrival of the notary with both marriage contracts, one of which he could not have anticipated needing, for the marriage of Rosine and the count, as forecast in Act IV, scene 1, was to have taken place at Figaro's house.

Throughout the analysis of *Le Barbier de Séville* we have often noted comic elements which, though only accessory to the action, are useful, either because they minimize tension through laughter or because they define the characters more clearly. Beaumarchais' understanding of the utility and limitations of incidental comic effects led him to exclude some of them after they were created. The original play consisted of five acts. When its first audience found this too much, Beaumarchais promptly canceled one act and trimmed the others. The most significant examples of suppressed material, much of which was intrinsically valuable, are examined in the notes, but we have omitted consideration of the two earliest versions—one a *parade*, the other a comic opera. [41] Not all the variants, however, have been preserved. Consequently nothing is known of a putative sixth act, mentioned by Beaumarchais in the *Lettre modérée*, in which Figaro and Bartholo discover, as they are beating each other, that they are father and son. Apparently this farcical development encroached too much upon *Le Mariage de Figaro* and was in any case superfluous.

We have not attempted to show systematically how Beaumarchais progressed to the definitive version of the play, but it is evident that the simplicity and purity of the lines are the result of repeated excision. It is also clear that a rapid development of the action appeared to him of the greatest importance, even when achieving this meant sacrificing ingenious comic effects. It seems, moreover, that this quality is also essential to produce in reader or audience an illusion of reality and unity; the artifices, chance interventions, and incredible oversights of the characters pass unnoticed in the brisk succession of incidents. Finally, it is again the rapid sequence of reversing situations which seems to assure just the degree of tension and of sympathy propitious to the "comic illusion," but with the necessary lack of psychological profundity. The precept which Figaro himself gives for the deception of Bartholo—*il faut marcher si vite que le soupçon n'ait pas le temps de naître*—applies also to the reader and the audience.

Briefly, the excisions resulted in a simplification of the characters, which manifestly enhances the comic effect by establishing among them the comic hierarchy already noted, and in the realization of a more distinct and direct line of development. One recalls that Beaumarchais insisted upon the priority of characters. It would be hazardous, however, to conclude that all of the modifications derive from the transformations which he imposed upon them. His *Lettre modérée* is, of course, a justification posterior to the final editing of the play and contradicts the predilection for complicated intrigue which the author asserted in the preface to *Le Mariage de Figaro* and in remarks made upon *La Mère coupable*. Still other motives may have asserted themselves, particularly a desire to purify his comic spirit more and more toward the condition of wit.

·3·

Le Mariage
de Figaro

We shall apply a similar method of analysis to *Le Mariage de Figaro,* again examining the expression, characterization, and action, particularly as these interact to produce comic effect. There will now, moreover, be an opportunity for fuller comparison and contrast of the two plays.

Act I

The principal sympathetic persons are presented in the first scene. Suzanne is new, but Figaro far from unknown. Beaumarchais' use of characters continuing from the first comedy imposes an important modification on the second. Now most of his main characters bear the weight of personal history and can no longer be represented with the simplicity appropriate to typed comic roles. Some of the differences in Figaro, indeed

49

the principal one, appear in this first scene. The title itself
emphasizes that Figaro, no longer the detached manipulator
of intrigue, is himself involved in love.

The badinage which follows Figaro's lyrical welcome[1] of
Suzanne has several purposes. It sets a tone of amiable bick-
ering which recurs often throughout the play. It suggests to the
reader that the threatened exercise of Almaviva's *droit du seigneur* is no matter for grave concern; this is, indeed, a means
of providing the sufficient, though not exigent, tension proper
to comedy. It exploits two kinds of "parasitic" comedy which
likewise will recur: the erotic overtone and the laughter of
happiness. The first contest between the lovers is joined as
Suzanne responds to Figaro's lyricism with a brusque objection to the room which the count has graciously given them:

Suzanne. —Elle me déplaît.
Figaro. —On dit une raison.
Suzanne. —Si je n'en veux pas dire?
Figaro. —Oh! quand elles sont sûres de nous!
Suzanne. —Prouver que j'ai raison serait accorder que je puis avoir
    tort. Es-tu mon serviteur, ou non? (I, 1)

Here is a kind of competition which Figaro never faced in
Le Barbier de Séville. Suzanne opposes Figaro's logic with
the veto of what seems capricious will, for she is not yet ready
to tell him the real cause for her aversion. As Figaro yields
without a struggle, logic is humiliated in his person. She continues, confounding reason in the name of reason itself, and
finishes her assertion of dominance with *serviteur*, the key
word in a usually empty formula of politeness. The affective
situation keeps this witty sport from being overstrained.

There ensues a byplay of gestures and imitations. As Figaro
presumably mimics the errands he names, Suzanne imitates
him, in words and probably in gestures, but her words have a
comic bite, for Figaro's terms change meaning in Suzanne's
utterance. Thus in the first scene of the play, as in the last,
Beaumarchais uses an echo technique. Exasperatedly, Suzanne
tries to suggest, without naming, the count's real purpose,
compliance with which is urged on her by Bazile, scornfully
labelled *honnête* and *noble*. Her leading question—"Tu croyais,
bon garcon! que cette dot qu'on me donne était pour les beaux
yeux de ton mérite?"—pointedly contrasts *me* and *ton*, sug-

gesting a distinction where Figaro has naïvely assumed community of interests. Little wonder that she exclaims, "Que les gens d'esprit sont bêtes!" And Figaro most of all. So she must tell him directly that the count proposes to claim his traditional privilege of the wedding night. Figaro is certainly of the *gens d'esprit*, even in this context, for he reasons that his good service to the count merits recompense, and he has assumed moreover that his master upon his own marriage had renounced the *droit du seigneur*. Both of his assumptions are logical enough in the abstract but in the present situation wrong, obtuse, *bête*. The clever manipulator is himself a dupe. So the contradictory terms are identified in Figaro's person, and, as usual, he bows to the assault of Suzanne's scorn while sheltering himself behind the indefinite *on*.

No sooner has Figaro sustained this ridicule than more comes:

Figaro *(se frottant la tête)*. —Ma tête s'amollit de surprise, et mon front fertilisé . . .
Suzanne. —Ne le frotte donc pas!
Figaro. —Quel danger?
Suzanne *(riant)*. —S'il [y] venait un petit bouton, des gens superstitieux . . . (I, 1)

Figaro here seems about to protest his amazement in lofty terms when he is interrupted by Suzanne's down-to-earth remark, emphasized by a purely physical verb. The sudden deflection of spiritual to physical is a frequently noted comic device. (See Bergson, *Le Rire: essai sur la signification du comique,* p. 117.) Taking the initiative again, Suzanne pushes her ribald suggestion further with *bouton,* signifying pimple but adumbrating the cuckold's horn.[2] Again Figaro is victimized, his own words having made this witty degradation possible. More important, however, are the clarification of the count's intentions and the gaiety of the lovers, which preclude any disastrous consequences from the danger they face. Both are full of confidence in themselves and in fate, able to conclude the scene on a note of affectionate teasing which mocks the threat of an invasion of their nuptial privacy:

Suzanne *(se défripant)*. —Quand cesserez-vous, importun, de m'en parler du matin au soir?
Figaro. —Quand je pourrai te le prouver du soir jusqu'au matin. (I, 1)

The erotic allusion, though obvious and laughable, is also artful. Parallel construction and alliteration emphasize the assimilation of *parler* and *prouver,* words of seemingly irreducible meaning. Even more, the erotic sense is given by the stylized permutation of the adverbial phrases of time. Here it is Figaro, outmatched through the scene, who triumphs, and, despite Suzanne's parting coquetry, he remains a satisfied and confident lover.

Actually, Figaro occupies in this play somewhat the position that Bartholo held in *Le Barbier de Séville,* though the two personalities remain markedly different. Now Figaro must defend what he considers his own. Suzanne's role is analogous to Rosine's; she is menaced by a passion to which she cannot respond, though, even more than Rosine, she takes the threat lightly. As the only important newcomer in the play, with no past, she can plausibly display an attitude more carefree than Figaro's. Indeed, Suzanne is the one persistently humorous (i. e., detached) character in the play, despite her involvement in the conflict. The count is now the adversary. His intent too resembles that of Bartholo in *Le Barbier de Séville,* since he pursues here a woman who does not love him and who is somewhat under his dominance. The antipathy toward him is aggravated by his being married to the graceful Rosine and, even more, by his scheming to injure a faithful servant, to whose ingenuity he owes his marriage. Thus from the beginning the sympathies of the reader are strongly directed.

As in the first play, a fundamental triangular scheme persists: Suzanne willingly gives herself to Figaro, while being coveted by the count. But the grouping of forces is necessarily different. Figaro is reduced to a defensive position, and thus gains the reader's compassion, while the count becomes predatory, a power against which there is no equitable remedy. If he is to be defeated, it must be by maneuvering. One may almost ask which is the principal character of the play. Beaumarchais himself seems to have hesitated; the abandoned title, *l'Epoux suborneur,* suggests the importance which he attached to the count's role.

As a point of departure in both plays Beaumarchais fixed abstractly similar but not at all identical dramatic schemes. The conflicting forces are symmetrically arranged; Figaro

is seconded by the countess, the count by that old rascal Bazile. But this symmetry does not persist, for the action has
a tendency, inherent though restrained, to deviate from pure
comedy toward sentimental drama. Of this more later.

Left alone, Figaro takes a disenchanted look at his position.
He now perceives "trois promotions à la fois," with their bene-
fits ostensibly distributed but actually for the count alone. The
irony with which Figaro unmasks his master's pretense scarcely conceals his own alarm. Toward the end of the speech the
old Figaro reappears as, rallying, he sees that he must gain
the initiative. The strategy which he envisions—advancing the
time of his own marriage, stalling off Marceline, harassing the
count, punishing Bazile, and pocketing as many "gifts" as he
can—reveals momentarily the manipulator of the earlier play.
But *Le Mariage de Figaro* has a more complicated intrigue.
It quickly becomes evident that the count has two more allies
in Marceline and Bartholo, and the original symmetry of forces
is broken up. Moreover, Marceline's pretensions contain a potential threat to the solidarity of Suzanne and Figaro, as well
as presenting to Figaro a continued nuisance and embarrassment.

The addition of Bartholo to Figaro's opponents seems no
great matter. Their first encounter resembles those in *Le
Barbier de Séville*, an exchange of polite ironies until *le gros
docteur*, unable to maintain his role, brings ridicule on himself in an outburst of impotent anger. [3] With this advantage
Figaro mercilessly touches old wounds, recalling Bartholo's
mule as well as his professional ineptitude. Again he plays his
favorite trick of reversing values by placing *animaux* where
one might expect *hommes*. This alone produces devaluation,
but the stroke is even more severe from Figaro's assuming
that the reversal originates with Bartholo himself, whose duty
presumably is to aid mankind. Plainly Figaro has lost neither
wit nor animosity toward his principal victim of the earlier
play.

Throughout this interchange Marceline has been silent, and
Figaro leaves the stage before she speaks. One may infer that
Figaro does not care to talk with her; it is worth noting that
the two do not meet again until Act II, scene 12, when Marceline presents to the count her claim on Figaro. Tactically,

of course, it is advantageous for Beaumarchais to keep them apart, so that Marceline may develop her part of the intrigue secretly to its fullest comic effect and so that the surprise of her actual relationship to Figaro, when it is revealed, may be the greater.

The scene which follows is adroitly linked to the preceding one. Like Figaro, Marceline first recalls the failings and fiascoes of *Le Barbier de Séville:*

Enfin vous voilà donc, éternel Docteur? toujours si grave et compassé, qu'on pourrait mourir en attendant vos secours, comme on s'est marié jadis, malgré vos précautions. (I, 4)

Twice within a few moments it is made clear that, much as he might wish to, the inflexible Bartholo cannot get rid of his past. Always limited by his self-esteem, again he is destined to be the deserving object of ridicule. Despite the rancor between them, Marceline and Bartholo do have common interests. As they rehearse the present situation, from a point of view different from that of the protagonists, the reader becomes better acquainted with Figaro's enemies. There is little to add about Bartholo, except that his malice gives him from time to time a kind of wit. It is Marceline who, despite Bartholo's disdainful and authoritative airs, takes the lead throughout the scene and forces his compliance with her plan. She has the initial advantage of being better informed; she has, moreover, clearly formulated desires and an end, even though an absurd one, in view. Beaumarchais' development of her character is paradoxical, indeed risky. She is witty, malicious, scheming. She uses several of Figaro's tricks of logic and repartee—yielding to reproach only to turn it to triumph, simultaneously saying "yes" and "no." She reveals energy and resilience. Yet she is in one way more ridiculous even than Bartholo. Ready to marry the doctor—father of *notre petit Emmanuel*—or Figaro, she is obviously a marrying woman at any price.[4] The woman who is overeager, like Congreve's Lady Wishfort, has always been a figure of fun. Of all the undignifying passions which prompt ridicule, this is one of the most prominent throughout the history of comedy. This obsession, of course, gives Bartholo several opportunities for devaluating pleasantries about marriage in general and Marceline's fading charms and infatuation

in particular. [5] These have, however, no deterrent effect.
Marceline insists on coming to the point:

Marceline.—Eh bien! n'en parlons plus. Mais si rien n'a pu vous
    porter à la justice de m'épouser, aidez-moi donc du moins à en
    épouser un autre.
Bartholo.—Ah! volontiers; parlons. Mais quel mortel abandonné du
    Ciel et des femmes? . . .
Marceline.—Eh! qui pourrait-çe être, Docteur, sinon le beau, le gai,
    l'aimable Figaro?
Bartholo.—Ce fripon-là?
Marceline.—Jamais fâché, toujours en belle humeur, donnant le pré-
    sent à la joie, et s'inquiétant de l'avenir tout aussi peu que du
    passé; sémillant, généreux! généreux . . .
Bartholo.—Comme un voleur.
Marceline.—Comme un Seigneur. Charmant enfin; mais c'est le plus
    grand monstre! (I, 4)

Here Bartholo's first slighting remark provokes retaliation.
The reader is to understand that each praise of Figaro implies
that the doctor is his opposite. Bartholo's *fripon* is a shrewd
and undeniable touch, but Marceline is able to counter it with
généreux. Then the two views are brought into sharp antithesis
in *voleur/seigneur*, two extremes of the social scale, though
here linked by juxtaposition and rhyme. Each, of course, in
his way is right, and the conciliation is in the person of Figaro
himself. Marceline seems to agree in part with Bartholo in
le plus grand monstre, but even this becomes a term of en-
dearment.

She now comes quickly to the point of her long preparation.
Bartholo is to help her marry Figaro despite the imminence
of his marriage to Suzanne:

Bartholo.—Le jour de son mariage?
Marceline.—On en rompt de plus avancés; et si je ne craignais d'éven-
    ter un petit secret des femmes! . . .
Bartholo.—En ont-elles pour le médecin du corps?
Marceline.—Ah! vous savez que je n'en ai pas pour vous! . . . (I, 4)

Marceline will not be diverted by Bartholo's cynical grossness
in reducing woman's "secret" to a matter of body only. She
presses on to state the secret: "la femme la plus aventurée
sent en elle une voix qui lui dit: Sois belle, si tu peux, sage si
tu veux, mais sois considérée, il le faut." This is her motiva-

tion, and Suzanne's. It makes them for the time implacable opponents. The complements which she uses increase in positiveness, but with *considérée* the oracular series comes out again to anticlimax.

Despite his pretended superiority, Bartholo accepts her plan, and Marceline emerges as the stronger spirit. Of course, he is seeking simple vengeance, and their triumphal unison at the end of the scene conceals a profound discordance of motives. In the last three speeches the conciliation of *épouser* and *punir* is made possible by their violently different meanings for *volupté*. [6]

Beaumarchais wasted no time in bringing the opponents together, and Marceline suffers her first defeat. This entire scene of polite knife play between Suzanne and Marceline is based on the recurrent insinuation that Suzanne distributes her favors between Figaro and the count. Were Suzanne less adroit or the play itself a melodrama, the resulting exchange of incivilities could scarcely be other than crude. But Beaumarchais wisely chose to give Suzanne an amplitude of personality which contrasts sharply with the constriction and rigidity of the characters who provoke ridicule. Suzanne is pure, even virtuous, but likewise witty and worldly-wise. Her poise cannot be seriously or long disturbed. Thus she excites not only partisanship with her cause but interest in her personality. She is the woman any man would gladly imagine his mistress or his intended. These are qualities often found in heroines of high comedy—in Shakespeare's Viola and Rosalind, in Congreve's Millamant, even in Shaw's Candida.

In the skirmish Marceline presses her accusation and Suzanne replies variously by allowing the calumny to fall harmless, by taunting Marceline with her overeagerness for a husband who does not want her, by returning to their source insults which are not valid enough, or witty enough, to be final. All this produces intense verbal interplay. A key word from one speech is taken up, usually with changed implication, in the reply, as with *amer (l'amertume), procure, façon,* and the dialogue is thus closely cohesive. Other terms are played off against each other, sometimes producing specious conciliation, sometimes ironic contrast. Such are *dame savante, vieux juge, innocent, jolie, respectable.* Each woman neglects

a part of her adversary's meaning, responding to tone only or
pretendedly yielding to the rival's reproach. Over all there is
the tension of feigned, external politeness, masking hostility.
Thus throughout the scene there is both dissociation of normal
unity and fusion into unexpected and unstable unity. Altogether
the scene is a defeat for Marceline. Suzanne retains her confidence, thus encouraging the reader to do the same, and Marceline is left to a foredoomed intrigue. Both women, of course,
are in error from ignorance, and when this ignorance is corrected in Act III, they become as fervent allies as they are now
enemies.[7]

It is a relief to pass to a scene in which Suzanne confronts
nothing more formidable than the aimless, precocious Cherubin, who, being in love with love, is an innocent cause of
trouble. The laughter which results is somewhat parasitically
comic. To be sure, Cherubin is clearly ridiculous; sighs and
rhapsodies are his native language. He freely confesses

> je ne sais plus ce que je suis; . . . les mots *amour* et *volupté* le
> [coeur] font tressaillir et le troublent. Enfin le besoin de dire à quel-
> qu'un *je vous aime*, est devenu pour moi si pressant, que je le dis tout
> seul . . . (I, 7)

This actually expresses a kind of automatism; it is epidemic
adolescence, a favored condition among twentieth-century
writers of fiction, which possesses Cherubin, and not an in-
dividuated will or a reliable logic. Yet Jean Hytier sees in Suzanne a certain disturbance before the page, which affects the
tone of her replies without her knowing it.[8] She too becomes
a bit automatist, and her mimicking of Cherubin's extrava-
gances has a note of defense in it. Even the strong-minded can
be somewhat unsettled by adolescent excess. Nonetheless, she
systematically mimics his complaints. This is simple raillery,
comic by definition, a verbal form of disguise, which will later
in the play become an actual tactic. Five times in this short
scene Suzanne echoes the young sufferer: *heureuse/l'heureux
bonnet, mon coeur/son coeur, elle m'écoute/Ecoutez donc
Monsieur, amuser mon coeur/amuser votre coeur.* This is
not returning insults, as with Marceline, but rather a height-
ening of Cherubin's own absurdity. The terms repeated have,
of course, different implications with different speakers, and
the discrepancies necessarily provoke laughter.

There are other causes of laughter as well. The erotic overtones of Cherubin's ambitious embracement of all women are,
though innocent enough, yet persistent. What would be men-
acing in a libertine, such as the count fancies himself, is in
Cherubin only amusing, like the ferocity of a puppy. Likewise
his particular passion for the countess presents an incongruity
often exploited in comedy. Cherubin's emotionalism is a kind
of parody of the countess', and the incongruity, though genuine, is based more on their difference in rank than on their
personal qualities.

Thus the scene presents a transposition to the comic plane
of Cherubin's instinctive drive, though, ironically, the actual
object of his pursuit on stage is not a woman but a ribbon. With
Suzanne he is anything but masterful. Suzanne's mockery, perhaps more severe than Cherubin deserves, brings out the irreconcilables which his automatism covers, though he himself
has no insight into his own confusion. Correcting his absurdity
is not at all the object of the scene. Doubtless the frivolity of
both characters suggests a generalized deprecation of values,
such as fidelity and deep feeling, normally associated with
love. Here Beaumarchais permits a sporting with gallantry,
and sexual energy is momentarily diverted into harmless by-
ways. Altogether, the laughter here, as elsewhere, is poly-
valent.

Scene 8 reveals another aspect of Cherubin's role throughout the play. He is at once a parody of the count and the obstacle which his master encounters everywhere in his path
and over which he is unable to triumph, despite his superiority. Cherubin is one more way of rendering the count ridiculous. In this scene he is the silent, unseen, and undesired witness. Unlike most hiding scenes, this one gives no attention to
the concealed observer's thoughts, feelings, and gestures. It
is enough that Cherubin is there, aided, as G. Michaud points
out, by a mute "character," the armchair. Three times in this
play Beaumarchais renovates the old farcical device of hiding
several persons in one place. Thus, maintains J. Scherer, he
creates a "third space" which, always discovered by embar-
rassed characters, is necessarily unstable.[9] Sooner or later
this character is projected from it, and each of these incidents
creates a momentary "peripeteia."

The comic effects of scene 8 are then preponderantly from
stage situation, but with the arrival of Bazile, who now serves
the count as he once served Bartholo, this oversimplification
is replaced by the normal interplay of action, character, and
dialogue. This is the only time when Suzanne and Bazile con-
verse alone, and, ignorant of an immediate situation which Suzanne knows well, he exposes himself at first somewhat as his
employer had in the preceding scene. Initially Suzanne dominates the battle. She avoids a direct answer to his question,
even though doing so invites the unwelcome allusion of his
next speech. She daringly brackets Bazile and the silenced
count as equal ill-wishers to Figaro. But Bazile is both tena-
cious and witty in his own right. Undisturbed by her indignation, he holds to his special meaning of *raisonnable* and plies
his cynical logic so hard that Suzanne is temporarily reduced
to angry outbursts. Bazile's logic, though effective, is, of
course, specious:

Bazile.—Désirer du bien à une femme, est-ce vouloir du mal à son
     mari?
Suzanne.—Non, dans vos affreux principes, agent de corruption. (I, 9)

Bazile pointedly ignores the moral sense of *bien* and *mal* and
makes them interchangeable. His disarming sophistry continues:

Bazile.—Que vous demande-t-on ici que vous n'alliez prodiguer à un
     autre? Grâce à la douce cérémonie, ce qu'on vous défendait hier,
     on vous le prescrira demain.
Suzanne.—Indigne!
Bazile.—De toutes les choses sérieuses, le mariage étant la plus
     bouffonne, j'avais pensé . . . (I, 9)

Here he manages to reconcile *défendre* and *prescrire,* and
more important, *un autre* makes the count's claim and Figaro's
identical. Similarly he reduces to nothing the contrast between
sérieuses and *bouffonne.* Thus Bazile in his logic approaches
the total comic illusion, as described by Chapiro *(L'Illusion
comique,* p. 51), in which all real distinctions are quite anni-
hilated.

It is difficult to see why Suzanne finds herself temporarily
defenseless against such pressure. But dramatically Bazile's
campaign, particularly his reduction to unity of contrariety
cherished by Suzanne, is valuable, since there has yet been

no proof advanced that Suzanne's fidelity to Figaro is secure.

At the moment the count breaks from concealment, comic effect again derives from stage situation and immediate embarrassment. The count's triumph and righteous indignation are short-lived, for the discovery of Cherubin himself confronts the count with a menace which he had not anticipated. Figaro could not have chosen a more favorable moment to force the issue of abandoning the *droit du seigneur,* for the count, though furious with Cherubin's vagaries which are innocence itself compared with his own intentions, must in self-protection act gracious and receptive. With this awkwardness impeding him the count becomes the center of an "ensemble," a recurring device in both plays.

Such scenes deserve some general comment. Typically the ensembles force one character to hold his own, if he can, against several. Usually the besieged character, at fault through his own folly, finds himself in a losing battle and becomes increasingly ridiculous, though the opposite condition and result are possible. It often happens too that the characters not directly implicated become, in effect, spectators, though not so well informed and free of understanding as those in the audience. The ensembles, moreover, like some dialogue scenes, often reproduce in miniature the oscillatory movement of the over-all action. One has an impression of dizzying changes of fortune, as if the comic development were reaching a peak of intensity, though the very rapidity of the reversals tends to diminish their actual significance.

Scene 10 is such an ensemble. The chosen victim is the count, but his discomfiture at the hands of a pack of assailants is not so complete as that suffered by Bazile and Bartholo in *Le Barbier de Séville.* The count is beset on two scores: Suzanne and Cherubin; and both lead to his embarrassment. He cannot refuse to crown Suzanne with the virginal toque which Figaro presents to him, a symbol not only of her purity but of his own as well. Figaro's plan of attack is basically ironical. In the name of the whole company he celebrates the count's heroic virtue in renouncing *un certain droit fâcheux.* This forces the count to reply that indeed the right no longer exists. Yet the count does not openly renounce it, and Figaro's praise of *la grandeur de votre sacrifice* emphasizes the fact that no overt sacrifice has been made. In the end it is the countess who saves his face. He can yield to her regard for the ceremony without at all yielding to his ironical opponents. Even so, being maneuvered into a public avowal, however meaningless, is a defeat for him.

The second phase grows out of the first. Scarcely has the count refused to pardon Cherubin than he is reminded of the virtuous and generous role he has just accepted:

Chérubin *(tremblant)*. – Pardonner . . . n'est pas le droit du Seigneur auquel vous avez renoncé en épousant Madame. (I, 10)

For all his trembling, there is menace in this speech. And even more in Suzanne's support:

Si Monseigneur avait cédé le droit de pardonner, ce serait sûrement le premier qu'il voudrait racheter en secret. (I, 10)

With the countess' unanswered question—"Et pourquoi le racheter?"—the assault is complete. The count is aware that too many people know too much about his conduct and real intentions, and he quickly yields to unspoken blackmail. Even so, he does manage, though he is soon to be frustrated, to rid himself of Cherubin and to twit Suzanne on the favors she has granted to his page. He does not, however, regain his full standing, for Fanchette, previously silent, insinuates what everyone knows—that the count's toga of virtue is transparent. The count prefers not to understand her allusion, but it waits for him, to bring him further defeat in Act IV, scene 5.

The final scene of this act has two purposes: to show Figaro still with the initiative, planning not only to frustrate his master's vengeance but to keep Cherubin on hand for his value to the intrigue, and to warn Figaro, through Bazile, that his battle is not won. For once, one of Bazile's proverbs is, as even Figaro admits, not only fresh but sharply applicable.

Act II

Structurally, the first scene of Act II firmly links to the main plot the secondary intrigue involving Cherubin and the countess. The page becomes a kind of rival of his master for the countess' affections. That such competition is possible and that so innocuous a character can repeatedly impede him are hints that the count's efforts are basically ineffectual. It would be unreasonable, however, to expect the countess at this point, fully informed of her husband's wandering attention, to take much interest in Cherubin, for all of Suzanne's generous report. [10] Here and elsewhere her attitude is anything but detached; indeed, except for the amusement of seeing her apprehensions to be worse than the reality justifies, her conduct is more consistent with sentimental drama than with comedy. She is at this point almost the type of the wronged wife, even before she has been wronged. It is no surprise that she sees her hope in hastening the marriage and accordingly becomes the main couple's faithful ally.

With Figaro's entrance the tone changes sharply. Believing the initiative his own, he is supremely self-confident, disposed to play the philosopher-tactician. Accordingly he transposes the purely human intrigue into general, even abstract, terms. Actually his theory, which is sound enough, is exactly that once expressed, with less wit and pomposity, in *Le Barbier de Séville:* "En occupant les gens de leur propre intérêt, on les empêche de nuire à l'intérêt d'autrui." But here he goes even further in pretending superiority to events and circumstances. For interests and persons he substitutes *possessions,* and for a time talks like a treatise on the passions. All this, however, does not quite mask his concern and his sense of conflict. For one thing such ironical euphemisms as *aimable, ardeur, possessions* are not deprived of their immediate relevance. For another, he does confess himself troubled by Marceline's daring, though she is not enough to disturb his over-all assurance. Finally, he enjoys sharpening his wit against the countess' annoyance: he diverts the verb *tourner* from the real subject, giving it two irreconcilable though similar meanings; he acknowledges his falsehood, only to turn it into a compliment for her.

After these displays[11] Figaro's plan signifies a resumption of his involvement. He can scarcely see—and the reader is only a little more perceptive—that one disguise may lead to several. He has no monopoly on such a game. Hoping for a triumph, Figaro actually prepares for himself and his ally the most painful situation of the whole play. Nor does he foresee that his anonymous note to Bazile will effectively exclude the useful

Cherubin from the intrigue. In his cleverness Figaro lays for
himself a double trap.

The next sequence of scenes is somewhat ambiguous. Ostensibly the action of disguising Cherubin carries forward the
plan which Figaro has just announced. It is easy, however, to
forget this in the interplay of characters. The total effect is a
diversion from the main to a subsidiary intrigue.

Suzanne's comportment and Cherubin's are fixed. She is the
scoffing, though not malicious, imitator, he the lover caught
between the impulses of his sentiment and his timidity. For
Cherubin embarrassment and gaucherie are unavoidable. Even
through these, however, enough appeal reaches the already unstable countess to make an impression. So she vacillates between susceptibility and the poise proper to her rank. All this
is richly expressed in the dialogue. For example, this exchange:

Suzanne.—Entrez, Monsieur l'officier; on est visible.
Chérubin *(avance en tremblant)*.—Ah! que ce nom m'afflige, Madame!
   il m'apprend qu'il faut quitter des lieux . . . une marraine si . . .
   bonne! . . .
Suzanne.—Et si belle!
Chérubin *(avec un soupir)*.—Ah! oui!
Suzanne *(le contrefait)*.—'Ah! oui!' Le bon jeune homme! avec ses
   longues paupières hypocrites. Allons, bel oiseau bleu, chantez
   la romance à Madame. (II, 4)

The ironic title and formal tone only emphasize Cherubin's
boyishness. His faltering reply and fumbling for a compliment
lead Suzanne to supply *belle* for his *bonne*. This situation permits him to accept the epithet as his own, but again Suzanne
unmasks him by imitation. At this stage the countess avoids
speaking directly to Cherubin, but her confusion is eloquently
revealed in her speech. It is now Suzanne, the only one with
self-command, who permits—almost orders—the page to sing
what he does not have the right to say, and the song provides
an interlude of sentiment.

In the disguising which follows, the tenderness is effaced,
and Cherubin is forced back into a child's—almost a doll's—
role. He is further degraded by the erotic overtones in Suzanne's remarks, especially in scene 6, on his prettiness. In
his final degradation he is on his knees, like an automaton,

before the countess, and once again the comic is transmuted into the sentimental. Cherubin finally declares himself, in speech rather than song, toward the end of scene 9:

Chérubin *(hésitant).* – Quand un ruban . . . a serré la tête . . . ou touché la peau d'une personne . . .
La Comtesse *(coupant la phrase).* – . . . étrangère, il devient bon pour les blessures? J'ignorais cette propriété. Pour l'éprouver, je garde celui-ci qui vous a serré le bras. A la première égratignure . . . de mes femmes, j'en ferai l'essai. (II, 9)

Despite her efforts to maintain distance by substituting *étrangère* for the *aimée* which Cherubin doubtless intended and by deflecting attention from Cherubin's emotion to the ribbon itself, the countess is plainly shaken. She has indeed kept the ribbon. And her hesitation after *égratignure* suggests further that this laborious deviation is intended to conceal her own sentiments. [12]

Thus Beaumarchais, following Marivaux, was able to derive comic effects from awkward sentiment. He makes it successively change its object and its application, and emphasizes the obstacles created by itself in groping for adequate expression. But the moment such expression is found, or almost found, the comic is displaced by the sentimental.

These scenes reveal Beaumarchais' difficulties in portraying the countess. The confident and adorable Rosine of *Le Barbier de Séville* yields to a forsaken wife, painfully aware of her predicament. The unhappy personal history thus hinted makes her not the most tractable material for comedy. Even so, Beaumarchais extracted advantage from this awkwardness. Since she recognizes here and later her own duplicity she escapes serious blame for her part in a not entirely innocent game with Cherubin. Beaumarchais skilfully used her uneasiness to render more probable her ready forgiveness of a repentant husband, and thereby avoids in the denouement any taste of bitterness. Though her attitude does much to mitigate antipathy toward the count, it still contributes to making him the outstanding dunce of the play. But this truly comic value in her role emerges later in the play.

The unexpected arrival of the count in scene 10 is almost calamitous. It produces a temporary reversal of the action.

Figaro's strategy suddenly recoils upon himself, threatening him with exposure and the countess with far worse. It is worth noting that the development from the plan of disguising Cherubin, though interrupted, does come to successful completion in Act IV, scene 5. Development interrupted and then resumed was indeed a favorite technique of Beaumarchais. Not only does it promote verisimilitude, but it has also the effect of linking widely separated scenes.

The crisis which begins in scene 10 shows Beaumarchais again placing his sympathetic characters in a predicament, only to rescue them in some surprising manner, to the increase of comic effect. Here the release of tension and the ensuing laughter of relief comes with scene 15. In the interval the action builds from wit into something like melodrama. For all his knowing that the count and countess are emotionally involved beyond the justification of actual circumstances, the reader cannot fail to be affected by the passion of their quarrel.

The tension starts mounting with an exchange that bears the external traits of comic fencing:

Le Comte.—Si c'est Suzanne, d'où vient le trouble où je vous vois?
La Comtesse.—Du trouble pour ma camériste?
Le Comte.—Pour votre camériste, je ne sais; mais pour du trouble, assurément.
La Comtesse.—Assurément, Monsieur, cette fille vous trouble et vous occupe beaucoup plus que moi.
Le Comte (en colère).—Elle m'occupe à tel point, Madame, que je veux la voir à l'instant.
La Comtesse.—Je crois, en effet, que vous le voulez souvent; mais voilà bien les soupçons les moins fondés . . . (II, 12)

Here is the familiar trick of identical words forced into different and partisan meanings. *Trouble* as the count uses it expresses suspicion; the countess returns the word as a reproach. The same is true for *occupe* and *je veux*. This is indeed witty warfare, but even their adroitness produces no real comic effect, for the characters are for the moment deeply moved, and the reader, even though he knows the issue between them less serious than they make it, is still sympathetically involved. The countess is forced to lie, but unwillingly and for a reason difficult to blame; the count, despite his transparent inconsistency, is genuinely concerned for what he thinks his honor. The result is high dramatic tension, and the ordinary procedures of the comic produce a bitterness which taints the laughter.

The desperation grows as the countess is cut off from retreat and the count furiously pursues his advantage. There is an interval of farcical comedy in scenes 14 and 15, but the embattled pair have no part in it.

In scene 16 the countess atones for her disingenuousness. Her anguish is real, and the reader feels it, even though he knows that she could, with sufficient boldness, have spared herself and avoided the risk of irretrievable compromise. So the reader also waits with delight for the revelation of Suzanne's presence in hiding, a revelation which suddenly turns the count from accusation to bewilderment and prepares for a renewal of deceptive tactics from the countess. These follow rapidly in scene 19, in which scene 16 is replayed in reverse. The count is further reduced to the condition of a suppliant, and the comic, somewhat attenuated, is re-established as the countess, aided by a Figarolike Suzanne, manages to adopt the mask and deny her recent emotions. There are stages in this change. At first the adversaries are equal:

La Comtesse.—Vos folies meritent-elles de la pitié?
Le Comte.—Nommer folies ce qui touche à l'honneur! (II, 19)

The immediate continuation brings defeat to the count, in the presence of a witness: "Tu as raison, et c'est à moi de m'humilier." Even here, however, the count does not directly humble himself before his wife and offer reparation. This comes soon:

La Comtesse.—. . . Ah! si jamais je consentais à pardonner en faveur de l'erreur où vous a jeté ce billet, j'exigerais que l'amnistie fût générale.
Le Comte.—Hé bien! de tout mon coeur, Comtesse. Mais comment réparer une faute aussi humiliante?
La Comtesse (se lève).—Elle l'était pour tous deux.
Le Comte.—Ah! dites pour moi seul . . . (II, 19)

Amusingly enough, the countess' pardon, though conditional in phrasing, is effective, since in reality she has nothing to pardon, and might properly ask pardon herself. It is this realization which gives to her words "elle l'était pour tous deux" a significance which escapes her husband.

The scene ends on a note of tenderness, modified by Suzanne's insistence on triumph:

Le Comte. — Mais vous répèterez que vous me pardonnez.
La Comtesse. — Est-ce que je l'ai dit, Suzon?
Suzanne. — Je ne l'ai pas entendu, Madame.
Le Comte. — Eh bien, que ce mot vous échappe.
La Comtesse. — Le méritez-vous, ingrat?
Le Comte. — Oui, par mon repentir. [13]
Suzanne. — Soupçonner un homme dans le cabinet de Madame!
Le Comte. — Elle m'en a si sévèrement puni! (II, 19)

Again this reminds one of Marivaux. The word of pardon so desired by the count has already been spoken; the countess would have to revise only the conditional phrasing. Actually, she shows her consent only in the form of doubt, thus partly denying what she grants, until she destroys, as if in spite of herself, all negation by extending to her husband a forgiving hand. Indeed, the countess has too much conscience to be at ease in the company she keeps, and this quality gives her an interest beyond that of the conventional wronged wife. For a moment the two masters play a game parallel to the servants' (I, 1, and IV, 1) without any perceptible difference in tone. It should be noted also that the servants enact a like reconciliation in Act V, scene 8.

Figaro's breathless arrival is not only too late to be of any use; it is actually an embarrassment to all except the count. In conformity with the always oscillating movement of the play the two scenes which follow, again "ensembles," show Figaro floundering in his own trap and his recently humbled master again becoming suspicious. Figaro knows only that Suzanne and the countess have confessed something; the count really knows little more. Both women are, of course, fearful that Figaro will say too much. There is played therefore a scene which reverses the silencing of Bazile in Le Barbier de Séville (III, 2). Here everyone urges Figaro to speak, always to his greater confusion; even his allies seem to turn against him. He tries several dodges and diversions, based on verbal hints (physionomie, mariage, consommé), and finally gets himself out of difficulty with his favorite device, at once admitting and denying:

Puisque Madame le veut, que Suzanne le veut, que vous le voulez vous-même, il faut bien que je le veuille aussi: mais à votre place, en vérité, Monseigneur, je ne croirais pas un mot de tout ce que nous vous disons. (II, 20)

Thus he shifts the burden of affirmation and decision to the others, including the count, who scarcely deserves the arbiter's role which Figaro pretends generously to yield to him. Since the countess wishes to keep her husband deceived, Figaro's specious gesture is safe enough.

But his slight advantage is offset by the new danger which appears with Antonio, and in the following ensemble he is again hard-pressed, not only by Antonio's blundering shrewdness but by the count and Cherubin's brevet as well. Most of the questioning is directed at Antonio, but Figaro is the object. Only good luck, exploited by Suzanne and the countess, assures Figaro's escape from Antonio's malign intentions. And it is a strain on the reader's credence that Figaro's simply knowing that the seal is absent from Cherubin's commission is "evidence" that it was he who jumped from the window.

Much of the laughter in the scene originates in Antonio's tipsy, bucolic acuteness. Though a simple and venerable device for comedy, Beaumarchais does not in other plays use the shrewd bumpkin as a character. Antonio is somewhat monomaniac, therefore somewhat automaton; for him, the bars are there to protect his beds, not the windows, and Cherubin was only something thrown from the window with disastrous effect on the gilliflowers. Such narrowness and his obvious inebriety make him seem at first no formidable opponent for Figaro. [14] But Figaro discovers that, though Antonio can be easily enough led into a diversion, he cannot easily be trapped. The count too has difficulty in making him follow a line of questioning. At first it does not appear that Antonio saw anyone jump from the window. But Figaro's attempt to capitalize on this, by claiming to have jumped himself, is ill-advised, for suddenly the *pleurard* rediscovers some memories which prove that he saw quite enough:

Antonio.—. . . Votre corps a donc bien grandi depuis ce temps-là? car je vous ai trouvé beaucoup plus moindre, et plus fluet.
Figaro.—Certainement; quand on saute, on se pelotonne . . .
Antonio.—M'est avis que c'était plutôt . . . qui dirait, le gringalet de Page.
Le Comte.—Chérubin, tu veux dire?

Figaro.—Oui, revenu tout exprès avec son cheval de la porte de Séville, où peut-être il est déjà.

Antonio.—Oh! non, je ne dis pas ça, je ne dis pas ça; je n'ai pas vu sauter de cheval, car je le dirais de même. (II, 21)

This makes the danger even more pressing. Figaro attempts another diversion, involving the fictitious horse, and Antonio seems to be led docilely into the absurdity and then to withdraw his suspicion. It is at this moment of triumph that, with a decent and considerate gesture, Antonio deals his shrewdest blow:

Puisque c'est vous, il est juste de vous rendre ce brimborion de papier qui a coulé de votre veste en tombant. (II, 21)

At this point all of Beaumarchais' skill is needed to save Figaro from exposure. Unaccountably, Antonio does not push his advantage, and the count does not act on his suspicions. Figaro's lame explanation and the absence of a seal on the document satisfy his master, and Figaro comes off unharmed, even somewhat triumphant. He does, however, suffer two losses: Cherubin is for a time removed from the intrigue, and the wedding, which at the end of the preceding scene appeared imminent, is postponed.

The count has long been awaiting Marceline. Her entrance then and her demand for justice appear the most serious threat so far. But again it comes to nothing. For reasons presumably of judicial dignity the count defers her case until it can be heard in form and further puts it into the background by losing his temper at Bazile. Indeed, by sending Bazile away on a humiliating errand he deprives himself of an ally he might have used against Figaro in the next act. With this crisis dispelled, the whole threatening situation relaxes into gaiety, and having promoted a song in his fiancée's honor, Figaro quits the stage, scarcely a conquering hero.

His insouciant exit may well have a further significance, for at this point Figaro's practical effectiveness toward achieving his desire comes to an end. The initiative passes to the countess and Suzanne, and Figaro is ignorant of their plans. His comic stature is thus diminished in two ways: he is henceforth in danger of becoming ridiculous, and his main characterizing quality—the identity of himself and the main intrigue—vanishes.

Act III

As Act III commences the count is preparing for his most extended contest with Figaro. His dispatching Pédrille on an errand is one more folly which is clear to all but the count himself, though the ridiculous results will appear only later. On
the other hand, the antipathy which the count provokes is somewhat reduced by the good resolutions which he announces in his
soliloquy. Yet these scruples are not wholly admirable, for
what the count really wishes is to learn from Figaro whether
or not Suzanne has informed on him. This time Figaro arrives
somewhat forewarned. The battle which is promptly joined is
actually an interruption of the main development of the play;
one of the results of the preceding act was to displace both men
from their positions as prime movers. Henceforward they are
more acted upon than acting.

Just at first Figaro takes the initiative by correcting his
master; he prefers *ma femme* to *la jeunesse*. This is a pre-
sumptuous anticipation, and Figaro is forced to retreat. Thereafter the pattern reverts to normal, with the count attempting
to extract information from Figaro by putting him in the wrong
and with Figaro using feigned humility or reasonable explanation as a mask for his counterattack. Thus in their first exchange the count's aggressive tone, expressing annoyance that
servants are taking over one of the privileges of masters, is
natural enough: "Les domestiques ici . . . sont plus longs à
s'habiller que les maîtres!" Figaro's reply—"C'est qu'ils n'ont
point de valets pour les y aider"—has the appearance of a
cheerful contribution to the count's thought, a kind of continuation. There is no denying the simple fact which he cites. The
effect, however, is the recoil of the reproach upon its origina-
tor and an amusing bit of social satire. Certainly the distance
between the social classes, here forced into momentary unity,
was greater in the time of Beaumarchais than it is today. The
degradation of greatness will be, however, appreciated in any
society—that is to say in all—which recognizes superiority and
inferiority, authority and obedience.

Somewhat the same thing happens when the count quizzes
Figaro about the alleged jump; here it is the questioner himself who provides the opportunity for evasion. An attack from

another direction is equally unsuccessful. The new diplomat
threatens to leave Figaro in Spain. This elicits no hint of a
comment about Suzanne. Rather Figaro contents himself with a
spectacular disquisition in answer to his master's objection
that he knows no English. Figaro's scornful discourse on the
language has nothing to do with the case, except perhaps to
cast discredit on the count's implicitly claimed knowledge of
English. The whole speech centering on the versatility of *God-
dam* is a typical comic reduction of complexity to a spurious
simplicity. In Beaumarchais' comedy it creates for the moment
a Kafkalike fantasy of frustration. No one ever gets what he
wishes in England, and nothing is desirable there. One futile
word suffices for the language and the country alike, as in
Shaw's *Saint Joan* the "God-dams" are the English soldiers
of Henry VI. It is not by logic that the count concludes from
this farrago that Figaro actually wishes to go to London and
that Suzanne has said nothing to him. Thus his second attack
fails, blunted by his own self-deception. Similarly, his insistence on knowing from Figaro why the countess should play
tricks on him gains him merely an accusation of infidelity.
The count has only himself to blame for having to hear the
disagreeable truth. [15]

Figaro's answer, as usual, is no answer at all, and even
the variant discussed in the notes fails to satisfy the count.
Hence his reproach:

Le Comte.—. . . Autrefois tu me disais tout.
Figaro.—Et maintenant je ne vous cache rien.

Far from clarifying anything, Figaro's response only repeats
his master's assertion; for a moment difference in phrasing
masks the substantial identity of the lines. Figaro's statement
is, of course, not entirely true, but only the spectator is aware
of what he is hiding.

Figaro continues to avoid any candid response by returning
to the *maître/valet* debate, a context in which he has already
scored significantly. It is surprising that the count would again
make a stand on this uncertain ground, but again he tries in
vain to cast discredit on *le valet*:

Le Comte.—Pourquoi faut-il qu'il y ait toujours du louche en ce que
    tu fais?
Figaro.—C'est qu'on en voit partout quand on cherche des torts.

Le Comte.—Une réputation détestable!
Figaro.—Et si je vaux mieux qu'elle? y a-t-il beaucoup de Seigneurs
    qui puissent en dire autant? (III, 5)

Here is a slight change in Figaro's technique: as usual he accepts the reproach in part, but he then extends its application
so far that the accuser finds himself accused. When the count
retreats behind public opinion, Figaro is able, generalizing
in turn, once more to make the *maîtres* inferior to the *valets*,
even in the eyes of the judge *(la réputation)* which the count has
invoked. Figaro's generality is only a mask for an attack on
his master whereby he returns the condemnation of "réputation
détestable" to its source. All comic effect would disappear
from his speech if *valets* were substituted for *Seigneurs;* there
would be left only a vapid bit of boasting.

Ignoring the personal application and pressing his accusation,
the count creates a misunderstanding of which he is himself
the victim. Once again Figaro discovers an advantage in the
count's reproaches and concludes with an unexpected—and un-
believable—renunciation of fortune hunting. This includes a rejection of any career in England, and with this the count,
though not seeming to realize it, is forced to reverse his attitude. In doing so he comes perilously close to revealing his
intentions, and to mask them he turns to praise: "Avec du
caractère et de l'esprit, tu pourrais un jour t'avancer dans
les bureaux." Figaro has conceded all reproaches so far. It
is consistent that he should reject this praise as if it were an
insult: "De l'esprit pour s'avancer? Monseigneur se rit du
mien. Médiocre et rampant; et l'on arrive à tout." This has
the added—and more important—effect of denying his adversary these commendable qualities. The satire, though general in expression, is aimed at the nobleman who is about to
commence a political career. Figaro now reverses the wit
by which he lampooned the English language. He could easily
reduce diplomacy to one word, "pretense." Instead, he develops this unity into a series of factitious contrasts, and
allows the count to supply the identity which brings them to
a point:

Le Comte.—Eh! c'est l'intrigue que tu définis!
Figaro.—La politique, l'intrigue, volontiers; . . .

Again the generalization discredits the count's own attempted adroitness, for in this very scene he has been systematically pretending false motives. This time the count can directly apply the generality to himself and infer correctly that Suzanne has revealed his true motives.

He sees therefore no further reason for concealment, and his question—"Ainsi tu espères gagner ton procès contre Marceline?"—may be taken as a threat forecasting his final threat of scene 5, that Figaro will marry Marceline. Faithful to his tactics, Figaro evades the issue and puts the count into the position of the accused. Figaro's response is technically polite, but the familiarity implied in *souffler*[16] and the third evocation of the *maîtres/valets* maneuver make it pointed enough to be felt.

The end of the contest hints that the count is planning an abuse of justice, with Figaro the intended victim. Thus Beaumarchais anticipates the tribunal scenes which are soon to come. [17] No more than a hint is desirable here, for to discredit the count's justice before the moment of judgment would be to rob that moment of its interest.

Both of the combatants triumph, the count because he learns what he wishes to know and Figaro because he manipulates his master's "convictions" at will, indeed achieves intellectual mastery. It is a hollow success. Figaro permits himself to think that there would be a gain in making the count accept two irreconcilable opinions. This shows already that control of the intrigue has escaped him. His triumph is strictly personal and verbal: he confuses his master but endangers his own wedding, and the advantage for future action lies with the count.

This advantage is soon undermined, but by Suzanne acting independently of Figaro. The brief scene (9) in which this is accomplished is one of the best in the play and the only instance of dialogue limited to the count and Suzanne. In view of the denouement, both propriety and psychological probability discourage more frequent intimate conversations between these two. Even the present scene is markedly artificial because of the credulity which emerges in the count's conduct. This, however, serves to emphasize Suzanne's innate cunning

and her impudence. Though ostensibly sent by her mistress,
she has come intending to promote a rendezvous for the evening, but she manipulates the count, who is at first somewhat
cautious, into making the proposal himself, and thus puts the
responsibility on him. The reversal which she effects, by
means of which each plays a dual role, provides the general
comic motif. Suzanne gives her mistress' vapors as a pretext
for her sudden arrival, and asks to borrow his vial of spirits,
which, if he wishes, she will return promptly. This is an indirect invitation to the count to express his intentions once
more, but he cautiously declines, by means of an ambiguous
remark which may be understood as a threat. Expatiating on
the social status of the vapors, she pretends not to understand,
and thus tempts him to a more direct attack. He promptly falls
into the trap and relieves Suzanne of an active, compromising
role. This is just what she wishes.

Le Comte.—Une fiancée bien éprise, et qui perd son futur . . .
Suzanne.—En payant Marceline, avec la dot que vous m'avez pro-
    mise . . .
Le Comte.—Que je vous ai promise, moi?
Suzanne *(baissant les yeux)*.—Monseigneur, j'avais cru l'entendre.
Le Comte.—Oui, si vous consentiez à m'entendre vous-même.
Suzanne *(les yeux baissés)*. —Et n'est-ce pas mon devoir d'écouter
    Son Excellence? (III, 9)

The adversaries leave their thoughts only half expressed,
and the reader has the pleasure of guessing the rest. Thus both
Suzanne and the count seek to keep open a quick retreat if
needed. Suzanne does indeed take an extra step by addressing
herself directly to the count, but it is more important that
by imitating his reserve she makes herself a comic copy of
him. Once more the count loses in this game of patience, as he
presses her to resolve the ambiguity in *promise*. In comply-
ing, however, she neglects, modest girl that she is, the condition of the promise and hence half the word's meaning. One
might expect the count to remind her of this by stressing the
different possible acceptations of *entendre*. And Suzanne, apt
pupil of Figaro, promises without actually promising anything,
for her consent is interrogatively stated and consequently almost negative. If she is ready to listen, it does not follow that
she is ready to obey. Rashly the count seeks to impose his

meaning on Suzanne's words and further enmeshes himself in ridicule. Instead of clarifying the situation as he hopes, he only reinforces the mistake which Suzanne permits him to entertain:

Le Comte.—Pourquoi donc, cruelle fille! ne me l'avoir dit plus tôt?
Suzanne.—Est-il jamais trop tard pour dire la vérité?
Le Comte.—Tu te rendrais sur la brune au jardin?
Suzanne.—Est-ce que je ne m'y promène pas tous les soirs? (III, 9)

Suzanne returns to the count the form of his phrases, but while his questions are real, hers are equivocations, for all that he understands them as he wishes. Contrast is hidden, from the count alone, by exterior resemblance. In addition, the *jamais trop tard* of Suzanne justifies in advance all of her betrayals, including that in the denouement. Possibly, too, this attenuated consent serves to relieve Suzanne's own conscience. Even if she does not keep the rendezvous, she has not exactly lied. In short, the adversaries agree only in appearance—and in the count's fatuous hope. Beaumarchais underscores the uneasiness of their accord by making the count pass from *vous* to *tu* and back as he feels uncertain or secure.

Toward the end of the scene the count's doubts return:

Le Comte.—. . . Cependant il y a un certain Figaro à qui je crains bien que vous n'ayez tout dit!
Suzanne.—Dame! Oui, je lui dis tout . . . hors ce qu'il faut lui taire. (III, 9)

This time Suzanne again seems to follow the count docilely, even repeating his terms, but in place of his doubt she must express reassurance. She succeeds, and again the similarity of form hides a duality of meaning. But there is something more, for actually the second part of her reply nullifies the first. In effect, Suzanne affirms that she has and has not spoken: if *tout* can be reduced to *rien* by the end of the sentence, *hors ce qu'il faut lui taire* may take the value of *tout,* by virtue of the beginning of the same sentence. In Suzanne's mouth, as in Figaro's, "yes" can be made the equivalent of "no."

The same trick, with a slight variation, is soon repeated:

Le Comte.—. . . Et, tu me le promets? Si tu manquais à ta parole, entendons-nous, mon coeur: point de rendez-vous, point de dot, point de mariage.
Suzanne *(faisant la révérence.)*—Mais aussi point de mariage, point de droit du Seigneur, Monseigneur. (III, 9)

Once more, despite almost identical phrasing, the conclusions are clearly opposite. The count is vanquished with his own weapons, but he does not know it. Apparently having promised everything, Suzanne has really promised nothing. And her adroit escape from his kiss is equivalent to her final refusal and the ultimate defeat of his plans.

Throughout the scene the count is led from peevishness to a kind of adolescent delight in his own success. Actually, of course, Suzanne deceives him from the outset, and in no other scene does she show such presence of mind. Upon the abstract comic scheme, establishment of contrast under artificial identity, is superimposed a richness of nuance which originates equally in the form and the content of the verbal exchanges.

Surprisingly enough after such brilliance, Suzanne endangers her prospects and Figaro's by her passing assurance, "tu viens de gagner ton procès." It is by chance that the count overhears this. But the artifice is overshadowed by the reader's sense of the obduracy with which the count enters the trial, in which his exercise of power might be decisive.

Though the trial itself is briefly deferred, the encounters which immediately precede it are so clearly preparatory that all four scenes may be considered a unit. Scene 15 itself, another ensemble, is rendered irrelevant to the outcome by the startling revelation which soon follows. Even so, the trial is by no means a divagation, for its result, seemingly disaster for Figaro and triumph for the count, forces the revelation of scene 16, which imposes a drastic alteration on what had seemed complete. The trial sequence is, moreover, rich in comic devices, which we shall examine in some detail, though we shall pretty much ignore the accompanying social satire, which would require a kind of historical exegesis beyond our intentions.

Scenes 12 and 13 serve principally to inject Brid'oison into the intrigue and through him to forecast the prodigies of judicature which are about to be performed. His name, of course, recalls Bridoie, the dicing judge encountered by Pantagruel. But even a reader ignorant of Rabelais would be at no loss; the *oison bridé* is a traditional image of the ridiculous. The whole of his conversation with Marceline is a travesty of preconceptions. Every utterance of his characteristic "J'en-

entends" shows that he does not understand, but no amount of correction from Marceline disturbs his confidence. Brid'oison can only repeat the formulas of his profession, without conceiving of their significance, so that in the face of the facts his affirmations are equivalent to negation, a refusal to listen to necessary explanations. Conversely, Marceline's harassed denials take on an affirmative value; she is trying to set matters straight and to avoid unjust presumptions against her.

But Beaumarchais apparently made it a rule that even the most stupid characters at times enjoy flashes of wit, and, at least in appearance, Brid'oison triumphs:

Marceline.—. . . . Quoi! c'est vous qui nous jugerez?
Brid'oison.—Est-ce que j'ai a-acheté ma charge pour autre chose?
Marceline *(en soupirant)*.—C'est un grand abus que de les vendre!
Brid'oison. Oui, l'on-on ferait mieux de nous les donner pour rien
    . . . (III, 12)[18]

Marceline's question reveals an insulting surprise, but Brid'oison replies logically to the literal question only, neglecting her tone and implication. She is no luckier in her second attack. Marceline is, of course, right, but Brid'oison, somewhat like Figaro, turns his argument into a personal, and for him justified, meaning for *abus,* which makes the laughter recoil on Marceline, who has furnished her adversary with an opportunity to vindicate himself when she wished to humble him.

Brid'oison's superiority vanishes with the entrance of Figaro, who belittles him as a man and as a magistrate, indeed treats him as he had treated Bartholo. Figaro's claim to be the father of one of Brid'oison's children, and Brid'oison's contented—almost thankful—acceptance of cuckoldry, is a bit of farce recovered from an abandoned version of *Le Barbier de Séville.* (See Lintilhac, *Beaumarchais et ses oeuvres,* pp. 248-50.) Taking the offensive, the magistrate in turn reveals his own cynicism and freedom from scruples. Imprudently Brid'oison avers his belief in the supreme value of *forme.* This Figaro readily grants, and then empties form of all content. By declaring Figaro to be in the right[19] Brid'oison in effect acknowledges his own nullity, as he previously acknowledged his cuckoldry. Figaro pushes his advantage by laying a trap, and Brid'oison's falling into it is only an example of his blindness to all but form:

Figaro.—Monsieur, je m'en rapporte à votre équité, quoique vous soyez de notre Justice.

Brid'oison.—Hein? . . . Oui, je suis de la-a Justice. Mais si tu dois, et que tu-u ne payes pas? . . .

Figaro.—Alors Monsieur voit bien que c'est comme si je ne devais pas.

Brid'oison.—San-ans doute. Hé! mais qu'est-ce donc qu'il dit? (III, 13)

As in his interview with Marceline, Brid'oison automatically agrees and so acquiesces in Figaro's suggestion that formal justice excludes equity, for he seems to concede the truth of *all* of the valet's sentence and thereby annihilates himself. Brid'oison in fact becomes a victim of form, for Figaro generalizes only the negative meaning which the other furnished him for *payer* and applies it to *devoir* as well. The absurdity, which equates *devoir* and *ne pas devoir,* is concealed by an artifice of pure form. Brid'oison's crowning fatuity is that he accepts the absurdity, when his profession demands that he detect fallacies. Figaro used a similar stratagem with *probité* in *Le Barbier de Séville* (III, 5) and Suzanne similarly bemuses the count in Act III, scene 9 of *Le Mariage de Figaro.* Indeed, the witty transformation of negative to affirmative is a frequent device in both plays, though it is employed in such varied situations that the repetition is not wearisome.

With such preparation, it is not surprising that absurdities deriving from real or feigned obsession with form dominate the trial itself.[20] Brid'oison reaffirms his allegiance, not at all shaken by Figaro, in scene 14, where one may properly infer the damaging equation *robe* = *forme* = Brid'oison. The theme is continued in the ludicrous contrast between Marceline's luxuriant name and Figaro's. To satisfy form Figaro adopts the "baptismal name" *Anonyme* and thereby playfully suggests that a legal action in which the defendant is nobody is impossible. The absurdity is masked by the physical presence of Figaro, but its effect is to travesty the suit itself and the concept of justice which takes it seriously. The travesty is continued in the famous debate over the conjunctions *et* and *ou*[21] and the related question of a *virgule* which is either present or absent in the promissory instrument. The heavy machinery of legal form labors to produce absurdity, with Bartholo pleading earnestly and Figaro in pedantic irony. And when the entire farrago concerning the true text is over, no one knows which conjunction is definitive and whether or not the contested comma exists. Moreover, the count's sentence ignores these questions in favor of an arbitrariness entirely his own.

The procedure is reduced to ridicule also by the verbal interplay in which Figaro is the consistent parodist. This is seen in the assimilation and separation of *payer* and *épouser*, several times repeated. Figaro also quite legitimately echoes Bartholo's terms and verbal formulas, such as *je soutiens*, giving them always a slightly different connotation. His examples, likewise, such as "ou *la maladie vous tuera, ou ce sera le Médecin,*" follow the pattern of Bartholo's but cast disrespect on the pleader and his cause at once.

The count's sentence itself, with its specious appearance of simple good sense cutting through obfuscation, is expressed in a forbidding juridical jargon, and thus creates another variation on the mania for form. Figaro has used the weapons of his enemies to discredit them. The count's judgment seems to acknowledge the validity of Figaro's defense, and yet he is sentenced to pay, in one way (which is impossible) or the other (which is disastrous), exactly as his emphasis on the *conjonction alternative*, taken simply as a verbal formula, implies. Though Figaro has been the wit-hero of the trial, his intrepidity recoils on him and he is the victim of ridicule. This is the clearer from the rapidity of his change from joy ("J'ai gagné") to distress ("J'ai perdu").

Though there is little resemblance generally between the work of Beaumarchais and that of Franz Kafka, somewhat the same pretentious obscurity of law and justice emerges in these scenes and in *Der Prozess*.

In order to get his hero out of his predicament, Beaumarchais resorted to the trick of recognition of consanguinity, a favorite device in comedy and fiction. Within the space of a few speeches his worst enemy becomes a loving mother, Suzanne's protectress, and the strongest advocate of their marriage. Beaumarchais presumably hoped that the reader would experience a similar revolution in his feeling toward Marceline, and he attempted to encourage the change by giving her what amounts to a sermon on woman's servitude to justify her previous conduct. But this transformation demands too

much of the reader. Marceline's forwardness in seeking a
husband and her maternal affections, introduced almost without
preparation, are too diverse to be reconciled even within so
comprehensive a term as "love." Insofar as she is a comic
personality, Marceline is a mistake, without convincing psychic
and emotional motivation. She plays two separate roles. Following the recognition scene she could disappear from the play
without serious loss to it, for her effectiveness likewise as an
aid and an obstacle is dissipated. Even providing Figaro with
an identifiable parentage adds little to his felicity and nothing
to the comic.

As one might expect, Bartholo, suddenly confronted with
family responsibilities, likewise presents difficulties to the
critical reader.[22] In marrying Marceline years after their
intimacy he falls into the trap which he had prepared for Figaro. But he escapes becoming ridiculous, for he complies—or
so he says—out of pity, remorse, and of his own free will.
Bartholo's reversal is as complete as Marceline's. And after
Act III, scene 19, the enmity between him and Figaro yields
and is presently replaced by amity. It is hard to believe that
his change is sincere; yet pretence seems equally unlikely.
As with Marceline there is insufficient support in the play's
rapid action for his reversal, and Bartholo emerges neither
comic nor ridiculous. The variants make it clear that both
transformed characters gave Beaumarchais trouble.[23] Neither
one can be explained by the impulsiveness which one accepts
in Cherubin or the naïve inconsistency of Fanchette.

Probably the metamorphosis of Marceline and Bartholo into
Figaro's parents was imported by Beaumarchais from *comédie
larmoyante* and sentimental fiction. He suppressed one convention of discovery, the call of the blood by which relatives
have an intimation of their closeness. To Marceline's ambiguous question, "Est-ce que la nature ne te l'a pas dit mille
fois?", Figaro's unequivocal "Jamais" is almost a gibe at the
convention. Beaumarchais did, however, retain the familiar
explanation of a child stolen by gypsies, and the reader may if
he wishes see in the projected marriage of mother and son
the hint of barely avoided incest which adds a sensation to
many sentimental comedies.

For all that the two characters lose comic status, they are

useful. They permit at least the laughter of released tension, and they facilitate an upsurge of action. The wit which they manifest from time to time, even after the change, makes it easy to pardon the lack of psychological verisimilitude which Beaumarchais permitted himself.

It is consistent enough with Marceline's new-found emotions that she embrace her son, but an artifice that Suzanne appear at that moment with the money to buy Figaro's freedom from the marriage which has been otherwise voided. Presumably Suzanne has been absent from the trial and the recognition scene in order to secure the money. For all its similarity to a scene from farce or melodrama, Beaumarchais was able to extract comedy from this confrontation, and by familiar means:

Suzanne *(se retourne).* —J'en vois assez: sortons, mon oncle.
Figaro, *(l'arrêtant).*—Non, s'il vous plaît. Que vois-tu donc?
Suzanne.—Ma bêtise et ta lâcheté.
Figaro.—Pas plus de l'une que de l'autre.
Suzanne *(en colère).*—Et que tu l'épouses à gré, puisque tu la caresses.
Figaro *(gaiement).*—Je la caresse, mais je ne l'épouse pas. *(Suzanne veut sortir, Figaro la retient.)*
Suzanne *(lui donne un soufflet).*—Vous êtes bien insolent d'oser me retenir!
Figaro*(à la compagnie).*—C'est-il ça de l'amour? Avant de nous quitter, je t'en supplie, envisage bien cette chère femme-là.
Suzanne.—Je la regarde.
Figaro.—Et tu la trouves?
Suzanne.—Affreuse.
Figaro.—Et vive la jalousie! elle ne vous marchande pas. (III, 18)

Inasmuch as Suzanne must be informed of the new situation, the scene is necessary. But it is the manner which calls for attention. Figaro is beaten and content, as he will be later. Suzanne, having expended energy in useless anger, suddenly is relieved of tension. These are the comic elements of the passage, but alone they would produce little better than farce. Again it is in the details that the real effectiveness is found. Playing on a double meaning, intellectual and sensory, of *voir*, Figaro gets the upper hand of Suzanne. Then he adopts his favorite attitude, admitting part of her reproach and denying the rest, all the while using his fiancée's terms, which thereby take on irreconcilable meanings. When Suzanne, more angry than mystified, resorts to violence, Figaro empties her slap of significance and transforms it into a testimony of her love. Likewise with *affreuse* (opposed to *chère femme*); Figaro turns the hostility which it expresses into its opposite. Figaro's tormenting nets him some playful revenge but also a mild ridicule as well in his joyous acceptance of her abuse. [24]

Hereafter Act III relapses into the mood of sentimental comedy, with Figaro weeping for joy, Bartholo softening, Brid'oison conceding his own denseness, and Antonio quitting the scene. Two happy weddings are in sight. With the discovery of scene 16 and its immediate consequences the main intrigue of the play is essentially at an end. The remainder serves to show the count corrected and restored to his wife. This is a new action, though it contains repercussions of the old.

Act IV

In its retrospection Act IV, scene 1, is a link between completed development and new. Figaro here realizes that it was more fortune than he himself which produced the present felicity. His exertions were largely in vain, but this will not prevent his further vain exertions, which will make him again vulnerable to ridicule. Even more now Figaro's one-time control of the intrigue is gone. Nor is he any longer the character who steadily causes laughter at the expense of others. Only his wit and verbal agility remain unchanged.

In this scene Suzanne and Figaro enjoy privacy for the first time since Act I, scene 1. With the threats to their union dissipated, they relax into a merry tenderness, again reminiscent of Marivaux. This mood is reflected briefly in Figaro's wit. Since love and fortune are traditionally blind, it is natural enough that he should transpose himself into the blind man's dog and indulge in playful self-depreciation:

Figaro.—. . . Pour cet aimable aveugle qu'on nomme Amour . . .
   (Il la reprend tendrement à bras-le-corps.)
Suzanne.—Ah! C'est le seul qui m'intéresse!
Figaro.—Permets donc que, prenant l'emploi de la folie, je sois le
   bon chien qui le mène à ta jolie mignonne porte; et nous voilà
   logés pour la vie. (IV, 1)[25]

This is a metaphor developed in the manner of the *Précieux*, with feelings objectified in material things and acts. Submis-

sion appears as *le bon chien*, constancy as *logés pour la vie*,
and there emerges an assimilation of life and love. Even the
indecency of Figaro's anticipation is more delicate than ribald.
This kind of affection, however, is scarcely in Figaro's vein,
and he soon returns to normal with a play on the idea of *vérité*,
brought on by Suzanne's questions. Again, he replies without
replying, until the final sentence of his longest discourse. His
method is to divide the idea of truth, commonly thought unified
and absolute, into a specious plurality which permits oppositions between what is true and what may be well believed. This
has the effect of emptying *vérité* and all concepts associated
with it—*folie, sagesse, mensonge*—of meaning. He does end with
what Suzanne wishes to hear, that the sole remaining verity is
his love. But his sport has made even this affirmation unreli-
able; the whole exchange reflects Figaro's accustomed humorous view of the world more than it does his fidelity. And this is
emphasized when, Suzanne having promised to renounce her
rendezvous with the count, Figaro uses her phrase, "ta bonne
vérité," and receives a reply as simple as his was equivocal:
"Je ne suis pas comme vous autres savants, moi, je n'en ai
qu'une."

Instead of setting off the banter again and permitting Suzanne
a similar development, Beaumarchais leads the dialogue back
to sentiment. We then find Figaro saying that nothing quanti-
tative can express love adequately:

Figaro.—Et tu m'aimeras un peu.
Suzanne.—Beaucoup.
Figaro.—Ce n'est guère.
Suzanne.—Et comment?
Figaro.—En fait d'amour, vois-tu, trop n'est pas même assez.
Suzanne.—Je n'entends pas toutes ces finesses; mais je n'aimerai
      que mon mari.
Figaro.—Tiens parole, et tu feras une belle exception à l'usage. *(Il
      veut l'embrasser.)* (IV, 1)

The play on adverbs here is a way of affirming the superlative
degree while denying its sufficiency in the present case. Suzanne's second straightforward statement of devotion does not
stop Figaro's sporting, though he does express his satisfaction
that Suzanne's veracity is a happy exception to what he has

established as the normal unreliability of truth. The full import of this scene is realized later, when, for all her protestations, Suzanne keeps her rendezvous with the count. Figaro might well congratulate himself on being an accurate prophet, but he forgets that it was he himself who propounded the notion of the shiftiness of truth. It is not difficult for the countess in scene 3 to persuade Suzanne to change her resolution. But Figaro, for some time ignorant of the resumption of the countess' plan, suffers the ridicule which threatens the ignorant.

With the reappearance of Cherubin, a secondary intrigue of the old action is renewed. It is evident again that the countess' feelings are more engaged than she pretends,[26] but the embarrassments which the page causes yield pure comedy, not closely related to the new action.

Like Bergson's jack-in-the-box Cherubin, after having deceived the others, is made to pop into view by the slow-witted Antonio. The destruction of the false identity, which never deceives the reader, makes the humor of the disguise reveal itself. For a moment the situation threatens a new defeat for Figaro. But a combination of the count's own servants proves embarrassing for the master instead. All the benefit he gets is a clarification of the morning's puzzle. As soon as he tries to press his advantage the situation is turned against him, chiefly by Fanchette's impetuous outburst. He intended to be the punisher, as indeed would be his right; instead he finds himself again crossed by a dependent, who seems to have the power of witchcraft over him. For her part, Fanchette empties *aimer* of the meaning which the count had intended, and her consent is thus in effect a refusal, even if the count submitted to her stipulation. Finally, the laughter is enriched by the erotic note which Fanchette innocently sounds. Antonio too turns against his master and in a speech full of confusion manages nonetheless to emphasize the erotic allusions, denounce his master indirectly, and make the wayward husband's embarrassment complete and self-acknowledged.

Figaro's appearance provides a welcome diversion for the count, but no real recovery of prestige. Even so, scene 6 revives the examination of Figaro in Act II, scene 21, even to the terms used. Again Figaro's unawareness of recent events puts him at such a disadvantage that his adversaries can treat

him like an object, holding him back from the wedding pro-
cession and belaboring him with questions and accusations from
the earlier scene. It is not until they think him hopelessly
entangled that they confront him with Cherubin. This confrontation itself is staged ironically in conformity with Figaro's
eagerness to start the wedding festivities. Four times he invites the girls to follow him, and at last Antonio artfully presents him with Cherubin as if Cherubin were one of them. It is
an adroit application of the humor of disguise. The count and
Antonio combine to keep Figaro facing the facts, and for a
moment it appears that the slippery one cannot this time escape. But the count himself unwittingly provides the loophole
by noting that Cherubin has already confessed to the much
discussed jump into the flowerbed. Figaro fastens on the literal sense and ignores the implication, which alone interests
his accusers. Perhaps Cherubin did jump; "je ne dispute pas
de ce que j'ignore." But Figaro might have too, though he
does not directly confess the act. Thus he drives a wedge
between the two parts of the count's intended meaning and
takes refuge in what cannot be disproved, though all know it
to be fantastic. Perhaps two jumps, perhaps two dozen—what
does it matter? And he dismisses the accusation with another
invitation to the girls, after a tour de force of impudence.
Actually, the consequences of Figaro's being caught and ex-
posed at this point in the action could not have been grave.
But this is beside the point. Here and elsewhere, Figaro's
dominant motivation is his resolution never to be in the wrong.
Between this and his habit of pretending to accede to all reproaches is an ironical tension which cannot fail to generate
the comic. He gives repeatedly an amusing manifestation of
the self-assurance expressed in such royal formulations as
je maintiendrai and *Dieu et mon droit,* a confidence which in
other ranks and contexts is sometimes heroic and sometimes
mad.

The count has in reality no more success with Cherubin.
He thinks to banish the page from sight at least for the evening,
unaware that this itself will involve him in more confusion and
that Cherubin departs enraptured with his lady's kiss. As a
punisher or controller of destinies the count is ineffectual.
All he can do, as he himself says, is to endure what cannot be

prevented. So he endures the festivities, at which he is an honored guest, his interest stirred only by the countess' letter, which Suzanne passes to him in Figaro's presence. As the letter is, of course, a fraud, it threatens both master and valet with ridicule.[27]

Preparation for the deceptions and corrections of Act V is interrupted by Bazile's claim upon the count's justice, ridiculous because made in ignorance of recent history. The ridicule heaped upon Bazile, with the approval of all present, is much more violent than that which Suzanne faced in Act III, scene 18, while she was uninformed. The feature of scene 10 is the duel of insults between Figaro and Bazile, an enemy he has previously overcome.[28] At several points their belaboring of each other is so nearly physical that farce seems unavoidable, though the wit mechanism is for a time that which Figaro always favors. Each pretends to accept the other's jibe, but actually returns it to its source. As the replies become more rapid, however, name calling replaces witty insult. Even here, the responses are rich in alliterative effects, echoes, rhymes, and spontaneous associations. Finally, as *un sot* matches *un écho* and *briller* is reduced to *brailler*, the game, in danger of becoming wearisome, goes to Figaro.[29] If we consider only the interrogative form of "Vous me prenez donc pour un écho?" Figaro seems to be denying Bazile's assertion. Really he does something more effective; he transforms the assertion into physical fact and turns it against Bazile. Bazile's absurdity is the echo response to himself. Figaro modestly pretends to be unnecessary; nature itself exposes Bazile's fatuity.

Following this somewhat artificial delay, Beaumarchais allows Bazile to discover the truth and forswear himself:

Tous (*Ensemble*).—Il est trouvé.
Bazile.—Qu'à cela ne tienne!
Tous (*Ensemble, montrant Figaro*).—Et le voici.
Bazile (*reculant de frayeur*).—J'ai vu le diable!
Brid'oison (*à Bazile*). —Et vou-ous renoncez à sa chère mère!
Bazile.—Qu'y aurait'il de plus fâcheux que d'être cru le père d'un
    garnement?
Figaro.—D'en être cru le fils; tu te moques de moi! (IV, 10)

Despite his protestations Bazile betrays his promise of marriage, much as he betrayed Bartholo's trust in *Le Barbier de Séville*. The rest of the exchange, after Brid'oison backs Bazile into a corner, is a continuation of the duel with Figaro, which is now closely related to the action. Statement and reply are linked by *père* and *fils*. These words ordinarily suggest similar affective values, but here just the opposite. Each is identified with *garnement,* but Figaro has the advantage in timing. Yet Bazile withdraws with some dignity, ending the game on a note of comic contrast:

Dès que Monsieur est quelque chose ici, je déclare, moi, que je n'y suis plus de rien. *(Il sort.)*[30]

Quelque chose, however little it may be, should represent a higher value than *rien*. Bazile seems to attribute the superior value to Figaro, at his own expense. Bazile's irony, however, is not completely successful; it is turned against himself by his being compelled to withdraw his bid for Marceline. He does not seem inconsolable, and this makes him more a type than an individual emotionally involved.

For all that they quarrel, Figaro and Bazile are brothers in wit; perhaps both are somewhat overendowed in this respect. Their methods of operation, though not equally successful, are much the same, Beaumarchais gained variety of presentation in giving essentially the same characteristic sometimes to one personage, sometimes to a pair.

Despite the fact that the characters disperse with everyone satisfied, as Brid'oison says, the reader knows that all are in some way deceived. And this state becomes more complicated before the final clarifications. Complications arise not only from the purposeful disingenuousness of the countess and Suzanne but also from the vulnerability of others. Figaro himself provides an excellent instance of the latter in scenes 13 and 14. He is self-satisfied from his recent success. His suspicions are without foundation. He has, moreover, adopted a superior attitude toward his own love, but he is unprepared to act in accordance with his own profession. He is thus open to ridicule, and it is this temporary disposition which enables Fanchette to victimize him, not any effectiveness of her own.

Marceline, of course, tries to warn her son against jealousy, but, playing Bartholo in reverse, he boasts of his own perspicacity:

Marceline.—Il est toujours heureux de le penser, mon fils; la jalousie . . .

Figaro.—. . . N'est qu'un sot enfant de l'orgueil, ou c'est la maladie d'un fou. Oh! j'ai là-dessus, ma mère, une philosophie . . . imperturbable; et si Suzanne doit me tromper un jour, je le lui pardonne d'avance; elle aura longtemps travaillé . . . (IV, 13)

Figaro's speech is a portent of ridicule; soon every significant word in it—*sot, orgueil, fou, imperturbable, pardonne*—will tell against him. He has set the conditions of his own exposure, and his patronizing address to Fanchette is the beginning:

Figaro.—Eeeh, . . . ma petite cousine qui nous écoute!

Fanchette.—Oh! pour ça non: on dit que c'est malhonnête.

Figaro.—Il est vrai; mais, comme cela est utile, on fait aller souvent l'un pour l'autre. (IV, 14)

Like Figaro himself, Fanchette knows how to disclaim responsibility and say yes and no at once. Figaro both underestimates and overestimates her *naïveté*, and this error only secures his discomfiture. When he claims to know what she is seeking, he is simply mistaken; when she speaks of the pin, he feigns knowledge which he does not possess. Therefore he is caught short when she logically asks him: "Pourquoi donc le demander, quand vous le savez si bien?" It is, indeed, difficult to assess Fanchette's awareness. Her mechanical, *verbatim* repetition of the count's instructions is almost clownlike. But, whether by intention or not, the words she repeats have an ambiguous effect. They fill Figaro with alarm and lead to his tragic posturing of the next scene. They promise the reader some amusing, and ultimately harmless, developments. How they affect Fanchette herself, if at all, is not discernible,[31] and perhaps not important.

Little is now needed to close the trap on Figaro and assure his gullible participation in the masquerade which is soon to be played out, finally to a joyous conclusion. Marceline has little trouble in debunking her son's woeful speech. Repeating his own words to him is an obvious parody, and the opposing

senses of the same words remain incompatible, though the
reader is inclined to accept the derisive attitude. Similarly in
the continuation:

Figaro *(les mains sur sa poitrine)*. —Ce que je viens d'entendre, ma
mère, je l'ai là comme du plomb.
Marceline *(riant)*. —Ce coeur plein d'assurance, n'était donc qu'un
ballon gonflé? une épingle a tout fait partir!
Figaro *(furieux)*. —Mais cette épingle, ma mère, est celle qu'il a ra-
massée! . . . (IV, 15)[32]

Marceline destroys the importance of Figaro's tragical gesture
and the weight of his words; the lead becomes a balloon, a
transposition speciously justified by the analogy between *gonflé*
and *assurance*. Hence the pin is both figurative and .concrete,
but either way a weapon against his false heroics. On this is
imposed another comic contrast, between the insignificance
of the object and the seeming gravity of the result. Figaro is,
of course, foolish to hold to the concrete sense alone, for he
thereby emphasizes the trifling cause of his concern. Unsuccessful in one attempt, Marceline then tries the ironic repetition of Figaro's own expansive speech in scene 13. But Figaro
does not now recognize himself in her parody; he refuses to
play the role he willingly assumed, and the phrase *ballon gonflé*
takes on another unflattering sense.

The remainder of Act IV is not markedly comic. Marceline
makes her son agree that a hasty decision would be unwise,
but this does not prevent his inviting new ridicule by going
himself to the rendezvous. It is somewhat difficult to believe
that the warning which Marceline proposes to give Suzanne
is needed to forestall tragedy; Figaro as the perpetrator of
a crime of passion is not to be taken seriously. The final effect
is to prepare the reader for a comedy of errors and corrections in Act V.

Act V

The first arrival in Act V is Fanchette. As she is one of
several characters who embody chance, her presence alone
on stage for a few moments emphasizes the ignorant and groping condition of most of the participants in what is about to
unfold. Seeing Figaro, she quickly hides, as will almost all

other comers. Since there are but two pavilions for hiding, the reader anticipates some overcrowding, and comic results similar to those centered on the armchair in Act I, scenes 7-9. Fanchette thus sets a pattern for the stage action of the other characters, except for the countess.

Despite his mother's advice, Figaro appears in scene 2 intent on preparing a ludicrous downfall for himself by bringing witnesses. It is mainly by chance, and thanks to Suzanne's disguise, that the count succeeds, from scene 6 on, in snatching from his valet the role of the most ridiculous.

No doubt it is natural enough that Figaro, left alone before events which he believes promise disaster, should meditate on life and his woeful part in it. In fact, as Scherer has pointed out *(La Dramaturgie de Beaumarchais,* pp. 70, 399), the monologue enables Figaro to escape for a time from his foreboding into self-pity mixed with humorous self-deprecation. So long a monologue close to the denouement is somewhat awkward. At this point Figaro's character needs no more definition, and the reader is certainly eager to see the sport which has been promised him. Perhaps Beaumarchais wished to prolong this anticipation and to include a concentrated passage of satire before the comic overflowing puts all seriousness to rout. We cite only the passages which seem to us subject to comic interpretation, omitting the censorious historical judgments which Beaumarchais expressed through his monologuist, Figaro's résumé of the action, and his purely philosophic and tragic reflections:

Parce que vous êtes un grand Seigneur, vous vous croyez un grand génie! . . . noblesse, fortune, un rang, des places; tout cela rend si fier! Qu'avez-vous fait pour tant de biens? vous vous êtes donné la peine de naître, et rien de plus. Du reste, homme assez ordinaire! tandis que moi, morbleu! perdu dans la foule obscure, il m'a fallu déployer plus de science et de calculs pour subsister seulement, qu'on n'en a mis depuis cent ans à gouverner toutes les Espagnes; et vous voulez jouter! . . . La nuit est noire en diable, et me voilà faisant le sot métier de mari, quoique je ne le sois qu'à moitié! Est-il rien de plus bizarre que ma destinée! fils de je ne sais qui; volé par des bandits, élevé dans leurs moeurs, je m'en dégoûte et veux courir une carrière honnête; et partout je suis repoussé! J'apprends la Chimie, la Pharmacie, la Chirurgie, et tout le crédit d'un grand Seigneur peut à peine me mettre à la main une lancette vétérinaire![33]—Las d'assister [sic–d'attrister?] des bêtes malades, et pour faire un métier contraire, je me jette à corps perdu dans le Théâtre; me fussé-je mis une pierre au cou! Je broche une comédie dans les moeurs du sérail;[34] auteur espagnol, je crois pouvoir y fronder Mahomet sans scrupule; à l'instant un Envoyé . . . de je ne sais où, se plaint que j'offense dans mes vers la Sublime Porte, la Perse, une partie de la Presqu'île de l'Inde, toute l'Égypte, les royaumes de Barca, de Tripoli, de Tunis, d'Alger et de Maroc: et voilà ma comédie flambée, pour plaire aux princes mahométans, dont pas un, je crois, ne sait lire, et qui nous meurtrissent l'omoplate en nous disant: *chiens de chrétiens!* . . . –Mes joues creusaient;[35] mon terme était échu; je voyais de loin arriver l'affreux recors, la plume fichée dans sa perru-que; en frémissant je m'évertue. Il s'élève une question sur la nature des richesses; et, comme il n'est pas nécessaire de tenir les choses pour en raisonner, n'ayant pas un sou, j'écris sur la valeur de l'argent et sur son produit net; sitôt je vois, du fond d'un fiacre, baisser pour moi le pont d'un château-fort,[36] à l'entrée duquel je laissai l'espérance et la liberté . . . Las de nourrir un obscur pensionnaire, on me met un jour dans la rue;[37] et comme il faut dîner, quoiqu'on ne soit plus en prison, je taille encore ma plume et demande à chacun de quoi il est question: on me dit que, pendant ma retraite économique, il s'est établi dans Madrid un système de liberté sur la vente des productions, qui s'étend même à celles de la presse; et que, pourvu que je ne parle en mes écrits, ni de l'authorité, ni du culte, ni de la politique, ni de la morale, ni des gens en place, ni des corps en crédit, ni de l'Opéra, ni des autres spectacles, ni de personne qui tienne à quelque chose, je puis tout imprimer librement, sous l'inspection de deux ou trois Censeurs. Pour profiter de cette douce liberté, j'annonce un écrit périodique, et croyant n'aller sur les brisées d'aucun autre, je le nomme *Journal inutile*. Pou-ou! je vois s'élever contre moi milles pauvres diables à la feuille; on me supprime; et me voilà derechef sans emploi.[38] –Le désespoir m'allait saisir; on pense à moi pour une place, mais par malheur j'y étais propre: il fallait un calculateur, ce fut un danseur qui l'obtint. Il ne me restait plus qu'à voler; je me fais banquier de pharaon: alors, bonnes gens! je soupe en ville, et les personnes dites 'comme il faut' m'ouvrent poliment leur maison, en retenant pour elles les trois quarts du profit. J'aurais bien pu me remonter; je commençais même à comprendre que pour gagner du bien, le savoir-faire vaut mieux que le savoir. Mais comme chacun pillait autour de moi, en exigeant que je fusse honnête, il fallut bien périr encore. Pour le coup, je quittais le monde, et vingt brasses d'eau m'en allaient séparer, lorsqu'un Dieu bienfaisant m'appelle à mon premier état. Je reprends ma trousse et mon cuir anglais; puis, laissant la fumée aux sots qui s'en nourrissent, et la honte au milieu du chemin, comme trop lourde à un piéton, je vais rasant de ville en ville, et je vis enfin sans souci . . .

Soon afterwards he wonders:

> . . . quel est ce "Moi" dont je m'occupe . . . maître ici, valet là,
> selon qu'il plaît à la fortune! ambitieux par vanité, laborieux par
> nécessité; mais paresseux . . . avec délices! orateur selon le danger;
> poète par délassement; musicien par occasion; amoureux par folles
> bouffées; j'ai tout vu, tout fait, tout usé . . . on vient. Voici l'instant
> de la crise.

Considered schematically, Figaro's tirade is formed of
variations on one abstract theme, which recurs often in the
play. Repeatedly there is an opposition between some pretended *grandeur* and Figaro, and always the contrast is resolved to his profit by his degrading the *grandeur*. First the
opposition is between Figaro's worth and the count's; then it
broadens to Figaro *vs.* people and governments. Finally almost
all Asia conspires to prohibit his comedy on the morals of the
seraglio. The theme is resumed, somewhat negatively, as
freedom of the press (and of Figaro) affirmed in words but
denied in deeds. Then comes a contrast which ends in the
identification of *honnête* and its opposite, and another between
honnête and *profit* as these are understood by "proper" people.
Finally, disgusted as in his similar monologue in *Le Barbier
de Séville* (I, 2), Figaro is forced to assert the value of his
old trade. Both monologues have the same pace, though in the
earlier play Figaro is less prolix and names only one *grandeur,* the republic of letters, opposing him instead of the conspiracy of ill-wishers he now fabricates.

There remain the principal oppositions and reductions of
detail which he elaborates in this framework. First as to the
count. It suffices to contrast his image of himself with what,
in his valet's view, his master is; the conclusion inevitably is
that only luck of birth gives the count his elevation, that he
has no cause for pride. The fact of birth being an identity
which covers all humanity, it sufficiently justifies for Figaro
the condemnation of all the superiorities against which he may
wish to measure himself, and permits him to conclude that
his merit has been depressed by injustice. Somewhat the same
effect of wise inclusiveness emerges from Figaro's phrase
"le sot métier de mari." With this also Beaumarchais warns
against taking the declamation too seriously; Figaro can still
judge himself. This is a useful modification. At this point the

comedy would scarcely benefit from a central character who has suddenly turned paranoid.

The mention of *métier* leads Figaro back to his varied occupations. Here is a sorry history. The accident of his birth and rearing rendered all his knowledge useless; the only employment which the count's prestige could secure for his *chimie, pharmacie,* and *chirurgie* was that of a veterinarian. Tired soon of grieving the beasts, he left off this occupation, a failure. His second attempt was to serve men via the theater, both of which suffer degradation by the association with his earlier calling. But to make his comedy fail there was required the whole force of the Mussulman empire, and these lofty, though infidel, powers are thus reduced to the level of a trivial play. In much the same spirit Figaro reviews his career in journalism, in which, as in the trial scene, he invited his own defeat, and the rest of his turbulent life up to the present. But with his turning his attention to "ce 'Moi' dont je m'occupe," the Figaro who is superior to events reasserts himself, and he is soon reciting a farrago of characteristics in which one image denies or degrades its neighbor: *maître* is denied by *valet, ambitieux* degraded by *vanité, laborieux* by *nécessité,* and so on to the negative conclusion, "J'ai tout vu, tout fait, tout usé." Thus in a varied career the end product of furious activity has been a kind of nullity which disperses the pathetic mood, so that even his final outcries are theatrical rather than real. Once more Figaro has dramatized his own life in words, with the same result as in the comparable monologue of *Le Barbier de Séville.* He becomes again for a moment detached and humorous. This is an effective prelude to the practical joke which is soon to be played on him.

This realization is, however, delayed to make Cherubin the first victim of the ambiguity effected by disguises, which is the source of the comic throughout this scene. The countess is forced to renounce herself in favor of the false personage that she has become; she strives, without succeeding, to play Suzanne's role. Cherubin in turn is replaying Act I, scene 7, with the difference that now the countess can hear his ardor expressed. Despite the fact that all Cherubin's statements rest on an erroneous premise, everything he says is in some way true and apposite. But the combination of disguise and error also strips all characters of their individual traits and almost reduces them to interchangeable objects. The count is in Cherubin's role of Act I, scene 7 and again powerless; Figaro is somewhat in the count's position. Only Suzanne can keep her identity. This interchangeability is amusingly exploited in the number of slaps and kisses, to say nothing of remarks, which here and elsewhere reach something other than their intended destinations and the number of misunderstandings generated. And with the characters' identities their moral natures tend also to disappear. All is deception, either perpetrated or accepted. A harmless amorality pervades the action, which more and more offers not the verisimilitude of the theater but the fantasy of the masquerade hall.

The intervention of the count in scene 7 gives a kind of resumption of Act II, scene 19. The comic aspect is grosser, for its condition is the scarcely credible failure of a husband to recognize his wife through a prolonged conversation. Here the masquerade atmosphere is a useful persuader. The count reaches heights of the ridiculous here. He is the victim of his own strategy, and courting he confesses his sins eloquently to his own wife.

This scene partly repeats that immediately preceding by a simple substitution of the count for the page. The slap which Figaro receives is a poor device to keep him outside the action, but it maintains the somewhat farcical quality and, lightening the tone of the conversation which follows, turns aside any moral deprecation of the countess. The comic effect of the dialogue owes much to the "asides" and the echoing carried out by Suzanne and Figaro, who comment from opposed though equally justifiable points of view. Thus the play moves through this scene on different planes within a single time sequence.

The main line of development, between husband and wife, is rich in irony and comic oppositions:

Le Comte.—Ce n'est pas pour te priver du baiser,   que je l'ai pris. *(Il la baise au front.)*
La Comtesse.—Des libertés! [. . . .] [. . . .]
Le Comte *(prend la main de sa femme)*.—Mais quelle peau fine et douce, et qu'il s'en faut que la Comtesse ait la main aussi belle! La Comtesse *(à part)*.—Oh! la prévention!

Le Comte.—A-t-elle ce bras ferme et rondelet, ces jolis doigts pleins
de grâce et d'espièglerie?
La Comtesse *(de la voix de Suzanne)*.—Ainsi l'amour? . . .
Le Comte.—L'amour . . . n'est que le roman du coeur; c'est le plaisir
qui en est l'histoire; il m'amène à tes genoux. (V, 7)[39]

In order to justify his liberties, the count pretends that his kiss
is only a completion of what Cherubin not long ago attempted.
Not even the count himself believes this. As he continues,
a new absurdity emerges; all the compliments intended for
Suzanne come to the countess by her presence. Unknowingly,
the count is both affirming and denying the physical evidence
before him. As he transposes the gaiety of Suzanne into the
fingers of the countess he goes even further in mistaking
the reality which he pretends to know well. He ends with a
specious contrast between love *(roman)* and pleasure *(l'histoire)*, which can be reconciled only in the heart. But both the
contradiction and the conciliation are immediately invalidated,
since the count actually finds in the same person, his wife,
what he pretends to have sought for vainly. This gives an ironical cast to the whole lesson he reads her concerning the
charms of variety, a lesson which the countess attentively
follows. Unwittingly the count pays his wife first in knowledge and then in money and jewelry for favors which he believes Suzanne has granted him. Thus he terminates with no
satisfaction the bargain specified in Act III, scene 9, which
has cost him so much effort. As he leads his wife gently to
the darkened pavilion he loses his last chance of escaping
ridicule.

One might expect Figaro in scene 8 to substitute himself
for the count and, animated by his unjust suspicions, render
himself equally ridiculous. Several good fortunes prevent
this. Suzanne takes her mistress' place, and Figaro recognizes her from the first, though he successfully pretends that
he is still deceived. Thus he is not actually caught in a venge-
ful attempt at infidelity. The scene takes up the theme of Act
III, scene 18, but with a reversal of attitudes. It exploits a
double misunderstanding, that entertained by Suzanne because
she does not know herself discovered and that feigned by Figaro. From this arise two logical difficulties: what is Figaro's
purpose in so needless and risky a game and how can one ex-

plain his joy when Suzanne makes herself known by some slaps in the face, since her identity is no surprise to Figaro? Possibly Figaro simply wishes to tease his fiancée, making her undergo the ultimate consequences of her disguise, as he hints in his unfinished aside, "Il serait bien gai qu'avant la noce. . . ." This would make Suzanne the victim of ridicule and himself no loser. Possibly Beaumarchais wished, by giving Figaro the good fortune of recognizing Suzanne, to clear the two of any suspicion of baseness. Perhaps, finally, Beaumarchais wished to accentuate the "beaten and contented" theme, itself intrinsically comic, and could not conveniently lead up to it sooner. None of these explanations is quite satisfying; the scene remains logically somewhat cloudy.

Even so, it has its comic moments, resulting chiefly from a kind of parody. After Suzanne reproaches him for lacking in *bonne grâce,* his kneeling and his protestations are doubly false, for the love he professes exists no more than the person he is pretendedly addressing in an inappropriately oratorical style and in an unsuitable place:

Ah, Madame, je vous adore. Examinez le temps, le lieu, les circonstances, et que le dépit supplée en vous, aux grâces qui manquent à ma prière. (V, 8)

Figaro plays at being ridiculous and thereby escapes the reality. The same might be said of his way of conceding the superiority of feminine ruses, after his deceiving Suzanne is abandoned:

Suzanne. —Allons, Superbe! humilie-toi.
Figaro *(fait tout ce qu'il annonce).* —Cela est juste; à genoux, bien courbé, prosterné, ventre à terre. (V, 8)

This debasement, verbal and active, is excessive to the point of being a refusal. In order to render this unmistakable, Beaumarchais concluded the terms of humble adoration with one so grotesque as to destroy the total effect. The association between word and action is even closer, and more unexpected, somewhat earlier, when Suzanne, asked for her hand, deals out her first slap in the face. A moment of ridiculousness and humiliation results for Figaro, and Suzanne continues "translating" other terms and ideas of Figaro into the same action. But he escapes much as he did in Act III, scene 17, by giving the gestures a meaning contrary to what is usual and clearly intended. The correction administered by Suzanne becomes the culprit's felicity, except that he is not the culprit she thinks him. Once more the usual values are upset, this time to Figaro's advantage. He regains dominance of the situation, and they join in a cozy conspiracy of laughter at the others who are still at odds.

The count returns in scene 9 at the right moment to assume the ridiculous part which Figaro seemed to prepare for himself. And it is the victim who gives the signal which brings on stage those who will witness his discomfiture. [40] The final humiliation, in scene 12 and following, is aggravated by his illusion that his adversary is reduced to nothing. Figaro's calm is a surprise to him and actually a defeat. But when the count reaches, as he thinks, Figaro's level of lucidity, a worse defeat awaits him:

Le Comte. —. . . Homme de bien qui feignez d'ignorer! nous ferez-vous au moins la faveur de nous dire quelle est la dame actuellement par vous amenée dans ce pavillon?
Figaro (montrant l'autre avec malice). —Dans celui-là?
Le Comte (vite). —Dans celui-ci.
Figaro (froidement). —C'est différent. Une jeune personne qui m'honore de ses bontés particulières.
Bazile (étonné). —Ha! Ha!
Le Comte (vite). —Vous l'entendez, Messieurs?
Bartholo (étonné). —Nous l'entendons.
Le Comte (à Figaro). —Et cette jeune personne a-t-elle un autre engagement que vous sachiez?
Figaro (froidement). —Je sais qu'un grand Seigneur s'en est occupé quelque temps: mais, soit qu'il l'ait négligée ou que je lui plaise mieux qu'un plus aimable, elle me donne aujourd'hui la préférence.
Le Comte (vivement). —La préf . . . (Se contenant.) Au moins, il est naïf! car ce qu'il avoue, Messieurs, je l'ai ouï, je vous jure, de la bouche même de sa complice.
Brid'oison (stupéfait). —Sa-a complice!
Le Comte (avec fureur). —Or, quand le déshonneur est public, il faut que la vengeance le soit aussi. (Il entre dans le pavillon.) (V, 12)

The initially striking feature of this exchange is the tone. Both contestants, determined for good but opposed reasons not to name anyone, reach for a stiff, official style, and thus is achieved a kind of comic contrast, a transposition of feeling to the level of public affairs. Not only is emotion officially denied, but an ambiguity concerning *la jeune personne* is introduced. Having been informed that Figaro's meaning is correct, the reader enjoys the count's confusion as he prepares to rush into the trap. Figaro prolongs the misunderstandings, evoking both his and his master's relations with Suzanne in such a way that his explanation applies almost as well to the count's relations with his wife. Thus the "mask" is formed which justifies the count's mistake. Once again Figaro exploits his favorite method of pretended consent. He recognizes the imputation but lets the count furnish the refutation, that is, establish the identity of *la jeune personne*. In effect, then, the count proclaims himself a cuckold. But his ignorance, though basic to the comic effect, is of no grave consequence, for no one shares it.

From now on stage action dominates as, one by one, all the characters are reassembled to face the count in preparation for, first, his punishment and then the general reconciliation. He is, of course, dominated by delusions of magistracy: "Or, quand le déshonneur est public, il faut que la vengeance le soit aussi. " And so it is; his desire is accomplished exactly, but with a target he has not anticipated. His first shock comes when it is Cherubin, not the countess, who is pulled out of hiding. This is the third time the count has, in effect, released his page from a confinement in which he wished to keep him. His exchange with Cherubin only makes explicit this contradiction and the specious justification for Cherubin, valid because of two meanings for *se cacher:*

Le Comte *(à Chérubin).* —. . . Que faisiez-vous dans ce salon?
Chérubin. —Je me cachais, comme vous l'avez ordonné. (V, 14)

Despite this check, which might have warned him, the count persists in his intention to judge, thus moving as if blind to meet his own ridicule. It is useless for him to discharge part of his vengeance on Antonio, for even so "public opinion, " as expressed by Antonio and Brid'oison, condemns him:

Brid'oison.—C'est Madame que vous y-y cherchez?
Antonio.—Il y a, parguienne, une bonne Providence! Vous en avez tant
    fait dans le pays! . . . (V, 14)

And again the count ignores a warning.

When Antonio in scene 16 makes Fanchette appear instead
of the countess he simultaneously shows Cherubin innocent of
the count's suspicions and punishes himself for having been
his master's ally. This is a variation on scene 14, with characters and the register of language changed. Antonio once
again strives to imitate genteel speech and treats his daughter
as *madame,* but his efforts, both of language and action, end
in nonsense.

The third instance of forced discovery, which produces
Marceline, is abridged. It is necessary to a full assembly,
but adds nothing to the previous occurrences.

Then the actual "culprits" appear without being summoned.
Moreover, the magistrate is reduced to asking pardon of those
who ironically kneel before him. The disguising is ended, and
the count finds himself suddenly overwhelmed with humiliation which has been long preparing. The wayward husband,
who has gotten no pleasure from his amorous exploits, receives forgiveness from his wife, and, moreover, from his
subordinates a pardon which he has not asked for. Figaro now
adopts the role of adviser in marital politics which the count
assumed in scene 7. The "echo" which the count complained
of at that time is now embodied in characters who assert their
presence and their will, whereas the earlier "echo" restricted
itself to negatives. In the renewed echo, a prominent device
throughout the latter part of Act V, all previous irreconcilables are blended, and with this return to the comic, the
count's punishment, less severe in realization than in threat,
comes to an end.

With accord re-established, the rest of the scene is a distribution of prizes more or less tangible. All are satisfied.
Even Brid'oison has the pleasure of hearing his typical poverty
of thought approved by a chorus.[41] All is prepared for the saucy
rehearsal of issues presented in the vaudeville. The heart of

the matter is best expressed by Suzanne:

> Si ce gai, ce fol ouvrage,
> Renfermait quelque leçon,
> En faveur du badinage,
> Faites grâce à la raison.
> Ainsi la nature sage
> Nous conduit, dans nos désirs,
> A son but, par les plaisirs. . . .

Before we offer our concluding generalizations about the comic style of Beaumarchais it will be useful to review the major differences between the two plays, with particular attention to characters and action.

Figaro persists as the main character, though marked changes are imposed on him in *Le Mariage de Figaro*. Beaumarchais got rid of the little daughter to whom Rosine sent bonbons. This detail, though trivial in itself, suggests that Beaumarchais did what he could to relieve Figaro of the weight of his own past. Indeed, the Figaro of the sequel seems a younger man, though in fact he could not be; he is as witty though less adept in maneuvering. His control of the intrigue is only partial; he is often on the defensive and does not always recognize his own role. The intrigue of *Le Mariage de Figaro* is a force which Figaro lets loose but cannot direct throughout, as he does in *Le Barbier de Séville*. Therefore he experiences failures and finds himself taken unawares. Often he is astonished by the maneuvers of other characters; even the count's courtship of Suzanne comes as a surprise to him. Most of his success, particularly material success, is due to chance and to other characters, chiefly the countess, who supplants him as the manipulator of the intrigue. Figaro learns too late that it is impossible to be at once a judge and a beneficiary of justice (IV, 15), and as a consequence he is no longer the creator of comic situations but rather a victim. He has also lost—or has not yet achieved—much of the serenity which made him masterful in the earlier play. Satire on social conditions and institutions, as well as on his superiors, comes more frequently and bitingly from his tongue.

Thus the second Figaro is more complex, beset by the dualities of common human nature, and correspondingly a less potent mover of the action. He remains, of course, a sympathetic character, but both the source and the quality of the sympathy which he elicits are different.

If the partial defeats fail to render Figaro ridiculous, it is because he disarms the reader by his willingness to admit errors (except when he is in contest with an enemy) and to withhold from forcing his point of view. Credit must also be given to his gay courage, his ability to detach himself from events once they are over, and his readiness to begin the battle again. Moreover, he shows a curious and altogether advantageous division in abilities. For all that he fails repeatedly in action, his wit and verbal agility remain unimpaired. Thus he is an unsurpassed entertainer, even in his defeats and follies.

The count, changed from his position in *Le Barbier de Séville* as Figaro's ally, is now his rival for Suzanne; three years of marriage have convinced the count that "nothing ages a man like living always with the same woman." He is, then, antipathetic and ridiculous exactly in proportion to Figaro's being sympathetic and comic. His position itself is contradictory. He is the authority over his valet, but as a rival in love to this inferior the count is at best his equal and eventually his inferior. This situation is, of course, rich in possibilities for social satire. The count's ambiguous and untenable position reminds one of Bartholo's in the first play, though the count's is further complicated by his being a wayward husband rather than a deluded guardian, and a rival of Cherubin as well.

Beaumarchais amuses himself throughout the play by maintaining the rivals schematically in alternating fortunes. If Figaro is altogether benefited by chance, the count is consistently abused by the same force. And his evil geniuses are those least offensive characters, Cherubin and Fanchette, whom he is ever finding in his path at the most awkward moments. Even inanimate objects seem to conspire against him. The armchair, a mute participant in Act I, scene 8, seems to know even better than Figaro how to tease its victim.

The count, however, is never so objectionable as Bartholo. He experiences moments of hesitation, as in Act III, scene 4, and his graceful acceptance of defeat at the end of the play does much to restore him to the standing he temporarily abdicated. His position of dominance afforded him the opportunity, had he so chosen, to impose more tyrannically than he does on his dependents. Even his attitude toward the vexatious Cherubin might easily have been more punitive.

On the whole the count is more humiliated than debased, and his chastisements are not severe enough to leave him permanently damaged. Better than any other, he illustrates Beaumarchais' propensity for giving his characters a dual nature, neither all good nor all bad, all intelligent nor all foolish. In this respect, as in others, the count reminds one of Figaro. Indeed, their social differences apart, they are similar in spirit and even more in taste, since they prefer the same woman. But his duality makes him a less than formidable obstacle to Figaro. Indeed, Figaro encounters no really intense opposition in either play; such would be inconsistent with the gaiety which prevails.

Suzanne doubles her mistress much as Figaro reflects the count. If hers is a role analogous to Rosine's in *Le Barbier de Séville,* she quite surpasses her counterpart. Suzanne is the only one of the principal characters who assumes a completely detached and insouciant attitude in the face of *present* dangers. Only she consistently causes laughter and brings none on herself, even when she is in error. She is also the only principal character who is a newcomer, and we are tempted to conclude that this in large part permitted Beaumarchais to endow her with such demeanor. It is by association with Suzanne that the countess becomes in part a comic figure.

To the complexity of the countess is due the most important difference in atmosphere between the two plays. Indeed, in his preface, Beaumarchais names her as the very center of interest. This seems, however, an overstatement, for were it true, *Le Mariage de Figaro* would be a drama rather than a comedy. Certainly Beaumarchais guarded against her becoming a tragic personage, despite her problems. Except for her confused attraction to Cherubin, she has too much presence of mind for any tragic rapture or suffering. She does not hesitate to take the control of the intrigue away from Figaro and become his competitor. She takes the initiative in the strategy of disguises and thus joins the comic, rather than the victimized, characters. And, though her position as a wronged wife is traditionally a weak one, she contributes directly to her husband's discomfiture and partial rehabilitation.

Here again passages from earlier versions of the play show that Beaumarchais first saw the countess as much closer to transgression than she is in the definitive text. This is consistent with the generally more sensual tone of his pioneering work. Thus she was once at a moral level much closer to that of her husband, and this in turn made her forgiveness only a gesture rather than the marked act of pardon which it became. Likewise, in the earlier versions ridicule of the count lacked moral significance; he was more clumsy than culpable.

Cherubin also serves as a means of embarrassing the count, but in quite a different way. After Suzanne, he is probably the character most rich in comic and ludicrous effects, even though they are uncalculated. In his precocious puberty he approximates a typed character to whom nothing important can happen. His primary occupation is to run after women, even Marceline. From this derives much of the mildly erotic atmosphere of *Le Mariage de Figaro*, which in itself predisposes the reader to laughter. The prominence, moreover, of two items of feminine equipment, the ribbon and the pin, in his role makes plausible a Freudian explanation of his conduct. (See Lalo, *Le Comique et le spirituel*, pp. 138 ff.) Beaumarchais himself pointed to a consistent interpretation in his preface. Cherubin, he noted, causes the women whom he pursues to feel a vague uncertainty about their own emotions. "On ne l'aime pas encore; on sent qu'un jour on l'aimera. " Thus he provokes a kind of innocent excitement, "un pur et naïf intérêt, un intérêt . . . sans intérêt. "

There is, however, more than this to the comic contribution of the page. Lalo suggests that when there is a confrontation of two characters, the first of whom arouses antipathy, represents authority, and poses as a corrector, and the second of whom is altogether inoffensive, the result will normally be the defeat and degradation of the first. In *Le Mariage de Figaro* the working of this mechanism has several aspects. All of the count's efforts to remove the page from the scene of action end in frustration; the page, through no initiative of his own, offers an "interference-in-series, " such as Bergson discusses. Moreover, Cherubin always reappears in somewhat

the same manner. Either he emerges from a hiding place
(I, 5; V, 14), or he appears suddenly from behind a disguise
(IV, 4, 5). Amusement is enhanced by the fact that it is always the count who inadvertently brings him back into the
action and thereby causes his own confusion. Beaumarchais
felt the page's artistic importance, though he justified Cherubin's part in ethical terms:

Mais, est-ce la personne du Page ou la conscience du Seigneur qui
fait le tourment du dernier, toutes les fois que l'Auteur les condamne
à se rencontrer dans la Pièce? Fixez ce léger aperçu, il peut vous
mettre sur la voie; ou plutôt apprenez de lui que cet enfant n'est amené
que pour ajouter à la moralité de l'ouvrage, en vous montrant que
l'homme le plus absolu chez lui, dès qu'il suit un projet coupable,
peut-être mis au désespoir par l'être le moins important, par celui
qui redoute le plus de se rencontrer sur sa route. [42]

Fanchette, the feminine counterpart of Cherubin, is the
center of a secondary intrigue in which the count is again the
unlucky rival of his page. His double failure produces double
ridicule. Fanchette's interventions provoke, in addition, a
special comic response. She is motivated entirely by compassion for Cherubin and bears no malice toward his master. But
she always manages to expose the count's misconduct before
witnesses. Her *naïveté*, then, is in effect a mask; otherwise
she is another type, laughable but invulnerable.

Antonio the gardener also belongs to the characters who
embody chance. To some extent he is a counterweight to Cherubin and Fanchette; he is Chance in the service of the count
and therefore an obstacle, though not formidable, to Figaro.
Indeed, because he is routinely drunk, sometimes to the point
of incoherence, he is at best a dubious assistance to his master. His constant intoxication adds a coloration to the comic
atmosphere; it justifies a gross outspokenness, which often
degrades the count and expresses the secret thoughts of characters who are better controlled. He speaks the language of
the rabble, in itself a comic devaluation of literary language.
Inevitably such a figure absorbs a great deal of ridicule, and
for this reason also his effectiveness as an impediment to the
principal couple is reduced. It might be expected that in earlier versions of the play Antonio's role, and the discredit

reflected from him upon the count, was more prominent.

In contrast with the others, Bazile did not undergo important modifications from his character in earlier versions; nor is his part much changed from that in *Le Barbier de Séville*. Despite his verbal wit, he is simply a double agent, serving opposite intrigues according to his immediate advantage. From Figaro's point of view he becomes a "counterobstacle," though not an ally, and therefore as a dramatic force neutral. Somewhat the same is true of Marceline, who is barely mentioned in the first play, and Bartholo, who has lost his position as antagonist. Both commence in opposition to Figaro, but the *coup de théâtre* by which they change, though convenient to the resolution of the intrigue, leaves them dramatically of little significance. We have already discussed the adverse effect of their conversion on the comic force of the play.

Brid'oison, finally, seems more a gratuitous means of satirizing eighteenth-century French justice than a character. Constantly stammering his infatuation with *la forme*, he sets a contrast between his ideal and his inability to express it, much less act on it. Justice is thus reduced to form, and form in turn by his speech to a parody. Now parody is normally comic, whether as a kind of devaluation or as a specious and unstable union of logically incompatible meaning and expression. Though not at all subtle, Beaumarchais' satirical device is entertaining enough. The variants reveal, however, that Beaumarchais reduced the number of Brid'oison's appearances, presumably to avoid repetition of what could not be made to yield variety and to reduce the recurrence of trial scenes. Beaumarchais imposed on his formalist fool the contempt traditionally felt for a complacent cuckold and thus brought him down almost below the level of personality.

It appears, then, that the characters of *Le Mariage de Figaro*, especially those with a heritage from *Le Barbier de Séville*, have all increased in complexity, except for Bazile and Bartholo. None, however, enjoys a sufficient detachment from events to be purely comic, except for Suzanne. Perhaps to overcome the dangers of involvement, Beaumarchais shows them steadily clever in repartee, even at the risk of making them copies of each other or of himself. This is part also of the refinement which he systematically substituted for the combination of sensuality and moralizing to be found in the earlier versions, particularly of *Le Mariage de Figaro*. Not all traces of the original blend of farce and sentimental comedy were erased, and there remain accordingly incongruities in characterization.

The increased number and complexity of characters lead inevitably to complexity of action; gone is the classic simplicity of *Le Barbier de Séville*. Even so, the main plot itself, as in all of Beaumarchais' plays, is another *précaution inutile;* possibly none of the added themes or situations was invented by the author himself. (J. Scherer, *La Dramaturgie de Beaumarchais*, pp. 19, 20, 33, 35; R. Pomeau, *Beaumarchais, l'homme et l'oeuvre*, p. 151.) The articulation of elements, however, is Beaumarchais' own. The main plot alone implies three obstacles to Figaro's desires—the count, Marceline, Antonio; only the count persists to the end. In *Le Barbier de Séville*, of course, Bartholo was the sole antagonist. In addition to the central plot there are at least three secondary intrigues (Cherubin-the countess, Figaro-Marceline, Cherubin-Fanchette). Consequently the main characters are forced to split their roles; the count's for example, is divided three ways. There are advantages to this complexity. Each secondary intrigue creates a center of interest and also motivates the actions of the secondary persons. Even more, the parallel unfolding of these subplots brings on plausibly certain "series-interference" and hence justifies the large number of incidents which contribute to comic effect. But the difficulty lies in disentangling the imbroglio without undue arbitrariness. Beaumarchais succeeds in this respect, except for Marceline, who in effect is abandoned as a dramatic force at the conclusion of Act III.

In place of the symmetry of character grouping in *Le Barbier de Séville* the later play has a skewed arrangement. For some time the count's partisans are more numerous than Figaro's. It is only Suzanne's energy and affection which keep a working balance. At one time or another all of the count's people desert to the opposite group, leaving him finally alone. But his is not at all tragic isolation. It lasts a very short time, for as the countess returns to him, so then do the others. The cycle is complete, the incidents of *la folle journée* ended, and

everything can begin again on a future occasion, say the marriage of Cherubin. The elaborate mechanism has revolved
without reaching a startling objective or producing a cata-
strophic change.

Beaumarchais understood that the comic is best served by
avoiding sustained, mounting tension. (See D. Romano, *Essai
sur le comique de Molière,* p. 99.) Accordingly he filled both
works with a spirit of play, with repeated surprises and free
tossing back and forth of advantage. But the constant reversal
of emotional attitudes, enhanced by continuous change in situations, denied him the opportunity for any subtle psychological
analysis. These rapid peripeteias tend to destroy each other,
and characters are thus reduced to attitudes, lacking in depth.
(See J. Scherer, *La Dramaturgie de Beaumarchais,* pp. 144
ff.) Incapable of being profoundly affected, they are free to be
as witty as they wish. This does not mean that they do not invite
the reader's partisanship or antipathy. Except for Marceline,
each character early in each play claims from the reader the
general feeling which he will prompt throughout, despite temporary deviations. Consistent with the pervasive mobility
which we have been describing there is an abundance of stage
movement, a result of the large number of characters and
their complicated interrelationships. This too serves to give
an illusion of rapidly moving action, which minimizes the
importance of the always impending and often postponed de-
cisions.

We have several times noted the embodiment of chance in
Cherubin, Fanchette, and Antonio. Chance as a causative
force is sporadically influential in *Le Barbier de Séville.*
But in *Le Mariage de Figaro* the entire play may be viewed
as a tissue of events, happy or unhappy, deriving from chance.
The beginning artifice, which makes all others possible, is
the assemblage of such diverse persons at the chateau, all
present with the count's approval. It is difficult to understand
his hospitality toward Bartholo and Bazile. If it is easy to
justify the encounters of Cherubin, the count, Bazile, and
Suzanne in Act I, the logic of the count's unexpected arrival
in his wife's apartment (II, 10) is less evident. And the over-
turning chair of scene 12, when Cherubin has every reason
to be motionless, is beyond plausibility, though the chair must

fall to provide the impetus for the succeeding scenes. Much
the same could be said of Cherubin's lost brevet and of the
convenient discovery of the identifying mark on Figaro's arm
just when something irrefutable is needed to prevent his marriage to Marceline. Indeed, the very revelation of parents
for Figaro suggests convenience more than it does probability.
These are, of course, the cavils of an analytical reader. Actually, the whole fabric of *Le Mariage de Figaro* is an improbability, the history of *une folle journée*. Few readers will find
themselves so repelled by the logical flaws as to reject the
play entirely. Trickery is expected in the theater, and Beaumarchais for the most part stays within the wide margin of
plausibility which may be allowed in a play whose title sets
the action apart from the ordinary. When improbability got
temporarily out of control Beaumarchais could still rely on
his skill in rapid action and dialogue to keep a theater audience
from any damaging scrutiny.

For much the same reason are readily acceptable a number
of passages, comic or witty in themselves, but accessory to
the action. Such are the irrelevantly clever endings of Acts I,
III, and IV. These as well as other speeches show the characters acutely conscious of their roles; they are authors and
stylists themselves, perhaps projections of Beaumarchais.
They seem often to stand outside the theatrical illusion and
view it with amusement. It follows that language itself, as the
characters use it, has an almost independent dynamic, in
dialogue and soliloquy alike. Some of the most brilliant duels
contribute little to intrigue or development of action; certainly
this is true also of the songs. Yet without these nonfunctional
bits the plays would be less rich in total comic effect. This
comic-in-language is a constant through the two plays. In
characterization and action, however, complexity is the prominent quality of *Le Mariage de Figaro* and simplicity of *Le
Barbier de Séville*.

·4·

Conclusion

The chief aim of our analyses has been to reveal the general and specific operation of the comic in *Le Barbier de Séville* and *Le Mariage de Figaro*. In this conclusion we offer a brief statement of the constants of Beaumarchais' comic style as well as several important ancillary practices.

If it is true, as Chapiro believes, that the comic is enhanced by distance from ordinary reality, the setting of the plays in a Spain that never was provides the first element of the artistic construct. In itself the milieu is credible enough, though certainly not commonplace for the original audience or for most readers since. As such, it is hospitable to events somewhat strange but short of the bizarre, the events of *une folle journée.*

The principal inciters to laughter are types traditionally associated with comedy: clever valet and maidservant, avaricious and amorous old man, parasite, wandering husband, wronged wife. Beaumarchais could rely on a predisposition to find them entertaining. Almost all of them have, some steadily and some sporadically, a sufficient assurance in the face of disturbance or threat. In both plays the lovers are basically sure of success. Those characters who experience reversal or frustration find it in their natures to be easily consoled. Not even Bartholo in *Le Barbier de Séville* or the count in *Le Mariage de Figaro* is anything like desolated by defeat. On the other hand, the unsympathetic characters tend to be morally ambivalent, wavering between decency and mischief. As such they constitute, except perhaps for Bartholo in *Le Barbier de Séville,* weak obstacles and excite neither strong partisanship nor antipathy. Altogether the characters lack psychic and emotional power. Not one of them is animated by a sentiment or passion profound enough to shake his entire being. Even genuine tenderness among them is rare, and when it appears the comic is briefly suspended. As a result their problems never seem fateful. The very constriction of the characters, then, contributes to the reduced tension and involvement normally favorable to comedy. The degree of insouciance, of course, is not uniform throughout the plays.

This insouciance, the attitude which we have called humorous, is clearest in Figaro, especially in *Le Barbier de Séville,* and in Suzanne. As Figaro's viewpoint is the dominant one, it is imposed on both plays, even on the last three acts of *Le Mariage de Figaro,* after he has lost his previous control of the intrigue. As the plays progress, to be sure, approval of Figaro scarcely remains constant, and at the denouements there is no such gratifying distribution of punishment to his opponents as one might expect in plays which provoke intense feeling. Even so, the differentiation between preferred and disapproved characters is sufficient to orient the laughter. In principle, the antipathetic characters alone can excite ridicule; the sympathetic ones are only comic. This principle is from time to time violated.

Ridicule seems to vary in the two plays with the degree of any character's unpardonable ignorance. This ignorance may be simple blindness to what should be clear, some denial of self, an inherent contradiction, or a character's refusal to play the role which he has assumed for himself. On the other hand, no major character is absolutely and sustainedly stupid. Even errors, which are plentiful, tend to result from following some discernible, though misguided, logic, as particularly does Bartholo in *Le Barbier de Séville*.

There are several characters who by the criterion just suggested would at first seem proper victims of unremitting ridicule. Such are the servants in *Le Barbier de Séville* and Cherubin, Fanchette, and Antonio in the sequel. Here, however, we perceive constitutional ignorance, a kind of unconsciousness, and they accordingly escape. In these characters is embodied chance—just as intrigue is identified with Figaro—and their interventions have unforeseeable effects alike upon the sympathetic and antipathetic characters. These *inconscients* reveal the share of personal freedom which Beaumarchais exercised in managing the action. Moreover, their immunity to responsibility is suggested by their at times closely approaching identity with insentient states, such as Antonio's intoxication, or with objects, such as the pins, bonnet, and ribbons to which Cherubin is reduced.

We believe, in short, that Beaumarchais built his characters through successive versions as variations on a few models. Upon reflection one sees, despite differences, important characterological links among them. His social position aside, the count resembles Figaro; likewise Figaro resembles Bazile. In another sense this is also true for Suzanne and the countess. Such a method, rich in possibilities for mockery of one character by his near-double, would be infeasible in any play based on a profound conflict. And these personal similarities facilitate the cheerful denouements, reconciliations in which nobody remains either repugnant or severely afflicted. The variants from the definitive text, moreover, reveal another uniformity in characters. All of them were in earlier versions coarser, more cynical, more given to erotic and ribald allusions. As they developed all were refined, became wittier and more alike intellectually. Hence it is not solely from caprice that Beaumarchais often allows a justly ridiculed character to escape suddenly from his trap by unexpected cleverness. Altogether, it seems that in his characterization Beaumarchais achieved a marked unity without losing the disparities which generate laughter.

In the movement of action also we have observed some constants. In both plays a similar pace is maintained by the sequence of reversals, whereby advantage alternates between conflicting characters or groups, and by recurrence of scenes which actually mark time despite seeming briskness within them. In both comedies it is desirable that action seem to develop swiftly toward the resolution, but in fact a real occurrence of such rapidity would be ruinous to either play. The dramatic issues and the emotional involvements of character are not sufficiently deep to sustain it. These alternations of fortune, both over long stretches of development and within single scenes, give an illusion of furious contest which pleasingly counterbalances the reader's assurance, almost from the beginning, that the favored cause is in no real jeopardy. When this zigzag method is followed within single scenes the reader is often treated to the delight of two strong contestants each striving to overreach the other; a momentary triumph for one almost demands an effective counterattack from the other. Such movement is remarkably analogous to that in skillful fencing: attack, parry and riposte, counterparry and counterriposte, and so on, through a conversation in steel, until, as a result of a slight error in defense or a slight superiority in assault, a touch is scored. Still other scenes present alternation between passages of more or less gratuitous amusement and returns to the action. The deviations have the effect of repeatedly postponing resolution without modifying the fundamental dispositions or purposes of the characters, and this in turn reduces tension and minimizes the gravity of whatever is at stake.

The variants show that Beaumarchais sacrificed many passages to achieve the seemingly feverish pace which, apart from its contributing to entertainment, masks several dramaturgic tricks, particularly the frequent intervention of chance. But he rarely excised a passage which offered zigzag movement. When he did so, it seems to have been to avoid some obvious repetition.

The rapid pace is partly justified by the uniform mental

structure of the characters. Since all of them are endowed
with wit, albeit sometimes eclipsed or misguided, it is plausible that their responses, in action as well as in speech, be
prompt, diverse, and productive of numerous incidents. This
and their already noted detachment conceal the frequent interventions of chance and permit the characters to amuse themselves in the very reversals of situations which they create.

This apparent rapidity conceals also a uniformity of processes and themes exploited to comic effect. The verbal expressions of these are diverse enough, but the constitutive
frameworks remain not only similar but usually traditional.
The frequent use of disguises is a good example. Basically
the device is simplicity itself, but Beaumarchais enriches it
by doubling, either in the same person (the count) or with
the help of two (Suzanne and the countess), and by dividing
it into fragments, as in the repeated disguising of Cherubin.
Such fragmentation is a convenient means of linking scenes
far apart in the text, and this in turn promotes a plot at once
unified and complicated. As much could be said of the way in
which Beaumarchais uses the time-honored device of a hiding
place, whether the easy chair or the pavilion.

Somewhat the same unity in variety results from those amorous intrigues leading to the ridiculous, especially those
involving the count and Marceline. It is in these that Beaumarchais most cleverly makes one character the comic shadow
of another or, conversely, splits up a single character into
contradictory attitudes toward the same activity. The count
particularly is from time to time caricatured in Cherubin and
Figaro; yet the count has a triple role in love—ardent admirer,
wayward husband and would-be seducer, and controller of his
dependents' affairs. Bazile and Figaro both have double roles,
reconcilable only by their witty agility. Narrow and determined
as any one may be when a given role possesses him, there
is not a major character in either play who is in the usual
sense integrated. Yet all are pretty much types. In the man-
agement of this delicate paradox of characterization lies much
of Beaumarchais' technical virtuosity.

The major characters are further given a kind of family resemblance by their desire to exercise legal justice over others.
Strictly, it is only the count who has a title to the role of mag-

istrate, and he fulfills his function with gusto. He pronounces
Figaro's sentence according to something like due process of
law. But the count also attempts to exert informally the same
magisterial power over his wife and Cherubin. Here, because
he is vulnerable to judgment, his efforts end in embarrassment for himself. And an extra twist of the comic is added by
Brid'oison, who is at once a caricature of the count and of the
count's justice. Other characters, however, with no better
than self-arrogated right, share the count's ambition for legal
authority. This is the sanction with which Bartholo attempts
to control and conquer Rosine and on which he speciously justifies his self-defeating precautions. Marceline demands a legal
remedy against Figaro. Even Figaro does not escape from
this mania; imprudently he wishes to judge and sentence Suzanne. Particularly in *Le Mariage de Figaro* there is a continuous aura of law and sanctioned proceeding. Even the *droit
du seigneur,* in the count's mind, has the status which its
name implies. Orthodox legality, however, exists in the play
to suffer defeat, for what actually prevails is the comic sub-
version of authority and the unprecedented, though superior,
justice which conforms to the desires of the sympathetic characters. This is one of the important respects in which Beaumarchais' contemporaries saw *Le Mariage de Figaro* as *une
pièce d'actualité.* And it is noteworthy that the unorthodox
justice which triumphs recovers in humaneness what it loses
in regularity.

If one examines details of logic and diction, one can also
discover constant practices. Insofar as all the characters are
witty, they share the techniques of Figaro, which can be reduced to a few typical maneuvers, appearing singly, alternately, or in combination. We have many times noted that Figaro
ordinarily succeeds in returning every reproach to its author,
having first pretended to acknowledge its justice. Often he
simply broadens the scope of the accusation in such a way that
his adversary appears its proper target. Other characters
also use this counterattacking method with some skill, notably
Rosine in Act II, scene 4, of *Le Barbier de Séville,* and Bri-
d'oison in Act III, scene 12, of *Le Mariage de Figaro.*

Another logical trick, very like the preceding, consists in
reducing apparently irreconcilable notions to a specious unity.

Again this usually strikes at the attacker and transfixes him with his own reproach, or at least neutralizes its intended effect. Suzanne alone is capable of beating Figaro at this game, as well as others, though Bazile is not far behind her. The opposite of this maneuver, reversing the clear sense of a meaning or dividing a single meaning into incompatible significances, is no less frequent. Figaro uses this to transform insults into compliments. Somewhat the same logic permits him to provide replies which are not replies at all. Whole scenes—in *Le Barbier de Séville,* Act II, scene 13, in *Le Mariage de Figaro,* Act III, scenes 5 and 9—are constructed around this pretense. Moreover, the device, as well as the others, can be subtilized by a character's replying to the tone rather than to the words of his adversary, and by answers, put interrogatively, which convey a nuance not only of questioning but of negation. As characters are more adroit in all these manipulations their detachment from events shows itself more nearly complete.

Fundamentally, all three kinds of tactical logic—generalization, fusion, and distinction of notions—rest on a single artifice. The witty character discovers a speciously justified viewpoint which permits him to disregard the norms of meaning and, for a moment, to adopt a convenient intellectual "mask." Also in the working out of any of these devices devaluation usually occurs—devaluation of one part of a divided notion or of the notions plausibly united, or of the victim of a counterattacking reply. This provides a comic pleasure which goes beyond the witty maneuver itself, though still dependent on it.

The notions which undergo one of these processes of logical and verbal transvaluation are not numerous. Some are persistent or recurrent enough to constitute implied comic themes. It is, of course, with Figaro that most of the transformations originate, and often he repeats himself. The important instances of specious assimilation are *vérité/folie; devoir/ne pas devoir; louer/blâmer; accueillir/emprisonner; hommes/animaux/insectes; rire/pleurer; bonheur/malheur; entendre/écouter;* and richest of all in satiric applications, *maître/valet.* It is worth noting that the count, under Figaro's influence, exploits *hommes/chevaux.* Contributions from Bazile are not so generous—principally *bien/mal* and *prescrire/défendre—*

though his skill is considerable. Within the range of such trickery lies his habit of manipulating proverbs, modifying them,
reversing their normal meaning, displacing their moral import as he wishes and according to his own convenience. Suzanne offers *gens d'esprit/bêtes;* Bartholo and Marceline together *seigneur/voleur: se débarrasser/épouser; épouser/
punir; mariage/marché.* Of the same general order of logic
are identifications only implied, such as *digne/indigne* from
Bartholo and *voleurs/gens comme il faut* from Figaro.

As with the assimilations, the forcing of single concepts
into opposite meanings or specious duality may be achieved
by insistence or implication only. Among those subjected to
this treatment are *charmant* (blame and praise, moral sense
and physical sense), *habile* (blame and praise), *estime* (opposed to *aimer*), *dire* (opposed to *justifier*), all from the fecund
wit of Figaro. The count contributes *la mort* (taken as a kind
of benevolent deity). *Savants* (blame and praise), *respectable*
(referring to age and to moral conduct), *écouter* (opposed to
obéir), *entendre* (opposed to *écouter*) are among the subtleties
of Suzanne. This game, like the game of spurious identifications, remains throughout intellectual and abstract.

Transpositions from abstract to concrete, a process often
emphasized in discourses on comedy, are, by contrast, rare
in the plays of Beaumarchais. Bazile does objectify injustice
as physical dissonance and accord as gold. Figaro causes lies
to pass over into the category of plants, and likewise truths
by his demonstration that verity is mendacious. For Marceline
Figaro's pride is a balloon, but the pin which pricks it reverts
to quasi-abstraction in becoming an instrument of moral correction.

Beaumarchais did not, of course, neglect other means to
the artful unification of disparities. Often, as we have pointed
out, he repeats a sentence form but with a radically different
meaning, or completes an interrupted sentence in an unexpected
manner. More external yet is consonance, including rhyme, of
accumulated words, a verbal trick perhaps imitated from
Rabelais. This device is used to advantage by Figaro and the
count, and Bazile, the music master, is professionally acquainted with it. The variants indicate that verbal consonance

was even more prominent in the early versions of Beaumarchais' comedies.

These processes of comic wit, however, are not comprehensive. In addition, the defeated adversary is usually pushed, perhaps but temporarily, into the ridiculous, and thus the response provoked by wit is fused with the somewhat punitive laughter of ridicule. We have, moreover, directed attention to the laughter of release or relaxation, of simple happiness, of erotic allusion. In brief, wit alone does not account for Beaumarchais' rich effects, even though it is basic and, as the variants suggest, became more and more Beaumarchais' guiding principle as he worked toward the final versions of his comedies.

The *tour de force* in each concrete situation consists in finding "masks" which will move the action along rather than break its continuity, no matter how tenuous this may have been. It is in this process that Beaumarchais' unfailing skill best shows itself. His characters transvalue the most common language, indispensable in ordinary conversation. Hence in part the impression of naturalness which his dialogue gives. Moreover, the steady change of perspective which results as expressions pass from one speaker to another assures a continuously tense intellectual interest and an illusion of rapidity added to the rapidity seemingly characteristic of the action. This repeated application of techniques of wit enhances the plenitude of the dialogue, because the recurrence of words, though with modified connotations, and of sentence patterns establishes a material liaison from speech to speech and simultaneously minimizes idle questions and responses calculated only to provoke the sparkling wit of another character. Attentive reading reveals, to be sure, that Beaumarchais did not always escape this tempting error. At times the count before Figaro, Bartholo before the count, Brid'oison before Figaro seem only foils. More numerous, however, are the scenes in which the contestants fence on equal terms until the greater capability gains the victory and the lesser defeat and ridicule. Thus the dialogue for the most part achieves its brilliance while yet contributing to dramatic unity, which was achieved only through the author's successive revisions.

Indeed, unity of elements is the principal quality of Beaumarchais' comic style. Characters, action, and dialogue operate reciprocally throughout. The characters as they are would scarcely be credible or effective in a different mode of action, and *vice versa*. Similarly, no other kind of dialogue could reasonably be expected from such characters engaged in such conflicts, while it is stage speech which defines both characters and action. With order thus emerging from the interplay of elements Beaumarchais could safely and felicitously introduce a delightful variety, particularly into action and dialogue. This variety is, to be sure, further controlled by Beaumarchais' adherence to two closely related principles of comedy, contrast and devaluation and the masquerade of logic wittily manipulated. These tend to be efficacious irrespective of time and place; the pleasure which he designed for his contemporaries is almost equally available to careful readers in the twentieth century.

We do not wish to leave the impression that Beaumarchais was a consummate technician and nothing more. It would, of course, be idle to claim for him Aristophanes' dedication to conservative principles or Molière's moral passion. But these are the grandeurs of comic history; a lower place may yet be dignified. For all the artificiality engrained in *Le Barbier de Séville* and *Le Mariage de Figaro*, both are concerned with a persistent human problem: how may power be distributed so as to satisfy the equity of the heart? The solution which Beaumarchais provides is romantic. At the beginning of both plays, power is, for the taste of readers or viewers, misplaced, and there is a threat that this power will be used in a way distressing to common sensibility. Actually it never is, and the menace which it offers is light. But the power and its potential do exist, and this is enough to engage the concern of those who wish to see a different disposition. The action of each play represents the conflict and the intrigue by which a satisfying redistribution is accomplished, and in the course of this, great pleasure accrues to the reader or viewer from seeing privileged injustice undermined. It is likely, of course, that the initial injustice will be so assessed more by sentiment than by logic, and it follows that the victors over it are not at all restricted to scrupulous tactics. Both Bartholo and the count are, slightly

to overstate the matter, burdened with an existential guilt
or wrongness which presumably licenses the reader to take
pleasure in such trickery against them as would be thought
outrageous if they themselves attempted it. The equity of the
heart—itself a paradoxical term—is a respecter of persons,
not of principles, and thus ironically resembles the irresponsible power to which in these plays it is opposed. All this
places *Le Barbier de Séville* and *Le Mariage de Figaro* in the
realm of romance, a land entrancing for many reasons, among
them that its code is founded on feeling. In this respect romance is a norm of human desire, fact and law at best irk-
some intruders.

It was the triumph of Beaumarchais that he effected a fusion
of romance and superb dramaturgic wit. The result was a
comic style rarely equaled in the history of a great tradition.

Notes

Introduction
1. See Félix Gaiffe, *Le Rire et la scène française* (Paris, 1931), pp. 120-44.

2. *Théâtre; Lettres relatives à son théâtre,* Bibliothèque de la Pléiade [Paris, 1957], p. 234. Hereafter all references to Beaumarchais' work will be, unless otherwise specified, to the texts of this edition, which for convenience we shall abbreviate to *Théâtre.* There is an amusing inconsistency between Beaumarchais' concern in this passage for *la décente liberté* and the license which he allowed himself in his *parades.*

3. See "Un Essai sur le genre dramatique sérieux" (1767), *Théâtre,* pp. 5-6 *et passim.*

4. Eugène Lintilhac, *Beaumarchais et ses oeuvres* (Paris, 1887). See also Ferdinand Brunetière, *Les Epoques du théâtre français* (Paris, 1896), pp. 320-21, and Gustave Lanson, *Histoire de la littérature française* (Paris, [1930]), p. 813 n. Lanson lists the following probable sources for *Le Barbier de Séville* and *Le Mariage de Figaro:* Scarron, *La Précaution inutile;* Molière, *Georges Dandin;* Sedaine, *La Gageure*

imprévue . . . ; Marivaux, *La Fausse suivante;* Voltaire, *Le Droit du seigneur.*

5. Félix Gaiffe, *Le Mariage de Figaro* (Paris, 1942), p. 31.
6. *Ibid.*, p. 32.
7. "Lettre modérée sur la chute et la critique du *Barbier de Séville,"* *Théâtre,* p. 151.
8. See David Victoroff, "Le Rire et le rêve," *Revue d'esthétique,* III (Juillet-Décembre, 1950), 265-73.
9. Charles Lalo, *Esthétique du rire* (Paris, [1949]), pp. 27, 32.
10. Marc Chapiro, *L'Illusion comique* (Paris, 1940), pp. 46-50.
11. Elie Aubouin, *La Technique et psychologie du comique* (Marseille, 1948), p. 121.
12. Lalo, *Esthétique du rire,* pp. 132-33.
13. *Ibid.*, p. 233.
14. Raymond Bayer, "De la nature de l'humour," *Revue d'esthétique,* I (Octobre-Décembre, 1948), 329-48.
15. Lalo, *Esthétique du rire,* p. 104.

Le Barbier de Séville
1. See Henri Gouhier, "Condition du comique," *Revue d'esthétique,* III (Juillet-Décembre, 1950), 301-9.
2. *Le Barbier de Séville,* ed. F. H. Osgood (Boston, 1913), p. 114.
3. A variant reads "Aux vertus qu'on exige d'un domestique *il y aurait des* maîtres qui *ne seraient pas* dignes d'être valets" *(Théâtre,* p. 754). This suggests that Beaumarchais sought for the respectful form of the rhetorical question. It is more adroit to let the count himself pronounce the condemnation of masters.
4. Elie Aubouin, *Technique et psychologie du comique* (Marseille, 1948), p. 108, and *Les Genres du risible* (Marseille, 1948), p. 55.
5. See note 1.
6. David Victoroff, "De la fonction sociale du rire," *Revue d'esthétique,* II (Janvier-Mars, 1949), 34-47.
7. A variant gives another version of the same portrait, making more explicit the contrast with Rosine: "Mignonne, pucelette, jeune, accorte et fraîche, agaçant l'appétit, peau satinée, bras dodus, main blanchette, la bouche rosée, la plus douce haleine, et des joues, des yeux, des dents! . . ." This is substantially repeated in II, 2, of the final version. It continues, however, thus: "Toujours vis à vis un vieux bouquin, à la vérité toujours boutonné, rasé, frisqué et guerdonné comme amoureux en baptême, mais ridé, chassieux, jaloux, sottin, marmiteux, qui tousse et crache, et gronde, et geint tour à tour. Gravelle aux reins, perclus d'un bras et déferré des jambes, le pauvre écuyer! S'il verdoie encore par le chef, vous sentez que c'est comme la mousse ou l'agaric, ou le gui sur un arbre mort. Quel attisement pour un tel feu! . . ." *(Théâtre,* p. 755).
This sketch of Bartholo has the merit of witty exuberance. It creates

a figure which is verbally more repellent but also a monster rather than a person convincing in dramatic conflict. The passage lacks the later reciprocal exclusion of terms and employs some which are rarely found. Beaumarchais astutely kept the most current verbal and adjectival qualifications and added others which give to the final version the piquancy of sonority side by side with incompatibility of sense.

8. Etienne Souriau, *Les Deux cent milles situations dramatiques* (Paris, 1950), p. 219.

9. Danilo Romano, *Essai sur le comique de Molière* (Berne, 1950), p. 139.

10. Guy Michaud has identified intrigue with the character of Figaro in *Le Mariage de Figaro,* but this is even more true in *Le Barbier de Séville* (see "L'Intrigue et les ressorts du comique dans *Le Mariage de Figaro, "* in *Mélanges d'esthétique et de science de l'art offerts à E. Souriau* [Paris, 1952], pp. 189-203.

11. Eugène Lintilhac, *Beaumarchais et ses oeuvres* (Paris, 1887), p. 244, calls attention to several omitted exchanges which have no direct connection with the action. In them Figaro's scepticism becomes cynicism, and moreover he anticipates the situation in *Le Mariage de Figaro.* Any one of these considerations would have justified abandoning them.

Le Comte. —Sur quoi jugez-vous donc que je puis cesser de l'aimer?
Figaro. —Sur ce qu'elle commence, elle à vous aimer de bonne foi. Sur le train du monde ne suffit-il pas souvent qu'une femme soit à nous, pour que nous cessions d'être à elle? On ne sait comment elle va, mais aussitôt que nous les tenons, pécaïre! il est presque sûr qu'elles ne nous tiennent plus.
Le Comte. —Non, Figaro, le trait est mortel, je le sais. Je suis percé à jour.
Figaro. —Excellence, vous savez qu'il y a tant d'animaux dont la blessure mortelle se guérit en les écrasant; je crains bien pour la pauvrette que l'amour ne soit un de ces animaux-là.

We note here a dual comic intention. The irrational nature of love permits identification of logically opposed ideas such as *cesser/commencer* and *tenir/ne pas tenir;* this is an outgrowth of a pure but too facile wit. But in what follows both the count and Figaro transpose the metaphor of love's wound in a fashion suggestive of the *Précieux,* although their tone is somewhat more vulgar. This manner is not consonant with that of the final version.

12. A variant allows Bartholo's reproach to degenerate into a satire on women, an offensive insistence which seems needless, since without it Bartholo says enough to resolve the initial misunderstanding in his disfavor *(Théâtre,* p. 757).

13. Henri Bergson, *Le Rire: essai sur la signification du comique* (Paris, 1896), pp. 135 ff.

14. The sketch could be prolonged at the discretion of the actors. The continuation originally written by Beaumarchais made a veritable grotesque of Bartholo:

La taille lourde et déjetée,
L'épaule droite surmontée,
Le teint grenu d'un maroquin,
La jambe patte et circonflexe,
Le ton bourru, la voix perplexe,
Tous les appétits destructeurs,
Enfin la perle des Docteurs.

(Théâtre, p. 758)

This portrait does not altogether agree with that given by Figaro in the final version. It makes the scene deviate toward burlesque and the characters tend toward unreality.

15. As for the "description," Bartholo in the variants sets *confrère* in relief and brings down on himself still another insulting mock name, *Porc-à-l'auge,* as his *oser comparer* provoked *Pot-à-l'eau.* The scene was obviously degenerating into a series of puns which not even the count's pretended drunkenness could justify. Moreover, the process is too rigidly repeated. Bartholo always commits the same mistake and provokes the same result. He becomes thus a pretext only for the count's abuse, and the dialogue loses its substance. In the final version Beaumarchais retained only the basic procedure of meaningful names for Bartholo (see *Théâtre,* p. 758).

16. In a variant the speech ends thus:

Le Comte. —C'est vous qui l'avez dit. Eh bien, avec les vôtres, il n'y avait qu'à vous laisser encore traiter les nôtres; la cavalerie du roi aurait été bientôt troussée!

(Théâtre, p. 758)

This was a worse than tiresome observation. The comic effect of the first sentence is destroyed by shifting the interest from the person of Bartholo onto the horses. Beaumarchais would have gained nothing by trying to transform the specious assimilation of the two arts into a real identification.

17. This part of the reply was once preceded by two sentences:

Le Comte. — . . . Je crains seulement que vous ne m'entendiez pas très bien; je ne parle pas tout à fait comme je le voudrais.
Rosine. —On le voit de reste.

(Théâtre, p. 758)

Basically this is a useless repetition, a new provocation directed at a Bartholo supposed more stupid than in the definitive version. Rosine too appears less perspicacious and, even worse, Beaumarchais fails to express the witty contrast between "spirit" and "letter" of the final version.

18. Beaumarchais used almost the same series of adjectives in *Jean Bête à la foire*—"mon grand-père paternel, maternel, fraternel, tanternel, sempiternel" (scene 9)—with a similar effect. Specious unification by

sound and other farcical procedures are prominent in Beaumarchais'
parades.

19. The variants accentuate the farcical character of the scene. The
count, after an abortive attempt, succeeds in kissing Rosine's hand, and
calls her, furthermore, by her name—an obviously unlikely mistake. He
then seems to yield to Bartholo's command to leave on pain of a fine,
which adds a realistic, but scarcely comic, note *(Théâtre,* pp. 758-59).

20. See Marc Chapiro, *L'Illusion comique* (Paris, 1940), pp. 79 ff.

21. In the variants Beaumarchais insisted even further on the momentary reversal of roles:

Bartholo. —Quelle obligation, mon cher!
Le Comte. —. . . J'espère avant peu vous convaincre que personne ne désire autant
    que moi le mariage de la Signora.
Bartholo. —Comment vous marquer ma reconnaissance?

                                     (Théâtre, p. 759)

These lines certainly intensify the ridicule of Bartholo and give the count
a clear-cut irony, but Beaumarchais may well have canceled them in
order to avoid making Bartholo seem worthy of sympathy.

22. In a variant of Act III, scene 6, the count forgets his false name,
Alonzo, and calls himself Palezo, an unlikely error in the circumstances
(Théâtre, p. 760). As a result he compromises a momentary advantage
and provides the reader with another instance of Beaumarchais' delight
in embarrassing his characters. The embarrassment, however, finally
lodges with Bartholo, who must once more ask the count's pardon for
having made an issue of Alonzo's inadvertence. Since Rosine must remain ignorant of the disguise, Bartholo must yet beg a lower tone of
voice. In short, Beaumarchais sought to introduce a supplementary deviation, but the device for getting the count out of his embarrassment
too closely resembles that employed in scene 2 of the same act. And the
motive for silencing Bartholo is soon to be repeated in silencing Bazile
(III, 12). Beaumarchais had then good reason for sacrificing an incident
of intrinsic comic value.

23. Lintilhac, *Beaumarchais et ses oeuvres,* pp. 242-44, quotes a
variant markedly different from the final version of the same scene,
much longer, but with a number of exchanges retained. In the definitive
text Beaumarchais omits all of Figaro's divagations in medical jargon,
perhaps because of too much resemblance to Molière's. He also sacri-
fices the amusing pairs of proper names (such as Methusaleh—Youth) and
the mythological evocations resulting from the notion that Aesculapius
was the son of Apollo. The retorts indispensable to safeguarding the
"mask" which deceives Bartholo have been retained. It is plausible for
him to suppose that Figaro wishes to swell the bill. Certain of the preserved speeches take on a different sense in the final text. Originally
Figaro's *mettez-vous à ma place* was a justification; he had to intervene
immediately. Now the speech comes later and refers to the career of

Figaro the writer. A play by Bartholo on *animaux/hommes* was canceled, only to reappear in *Le Mariage de Figaro*, Act I, scene 3. After the mention of bonbons sent to Figaro's little girl the text is not only abridged but modified to increase comic effect. Here is the variant:

> Bartholo.–Vous vous mêlez de trop de choses, Monsieur!
> Figaro.–Que vous en chaut, Monsieur, si je m'en démêle?
> Bartholo.–Et tout ceci pourrait bien mal finir, Monsieur!
> Figaro.–Oui, pour ceux qui menacent les autres, Monsieur!

Bartholo's irony appears only in the contrast of polite tone and implied threat, and Figaro's replies, exactly in the same tone, simply return the threat. The text gains in "polyvalence" if Bartholo associates the irony of tone with that of terms susceptible of double meaning. Figaro is then in a position to adopt his standard tactic, transforming the reproach into praise and thus obliging Bartholo to abandon his advantage.

24. We omit detailed consideration of the long variant in which Figaro recalls his unrecognized merit as a dramatic author *(Théâtre,* p. 762). So far as action goes, the principal purpose of the scene is to let Figaro know what he needs about the key. In the final version the same end is achieved simply by getting Bartholo briefly off stage. The omitted text is full of incidental comic effects, as Figaro vies with Bazile (and the nephew of Rameau) in imitative sonorities.

25. See Jacques Scherer, *La Dramaturgie de Beaumarchais* (Paris, 1954), p. 149.

26. According to Lintilhac, *Beaumarchais et ses oeuvres*, p. 215, scene 12 once terminated quite differently. After the departure of Bazile the count confesses to Bartholo that his coadjutor is not at all sick. But Bartholo has just confidently diagnosed the illness, which moreover served as a pretext for his welcoming the count, alias Alonzo. The effect of this is to turn Bartholo in every direction at once, depriving him of all consistency and the action of all its tension.

27. *Ibid.*, pp. 216-17, cites a long variant of the same passage. We reproduce only a few speeches from it. To Bartholo's question Bazile responds, giving himself as an example:

Bazile.–Ma foi, non, Docteur; trop pauvre pour nourrir une femme, et pas assez riche pour nourrir une maîtresse, je me suis fait sage de mon métier et jeté dans le rigorisme. Mais je n'en sais pas moins qu'en toute espèce de biens, posséder est peu de chose, et c'est jouir qui rend heureux! Mon avis est que possession sans amour n'est qu'une obsession misérable et sujette á des conséquences . . .
Bartholo.–Vous craindriez les accidents?
Bazile.–Hé, Hé, Monsieur, . . . on en voit beaucoup cette année, m'a dit la vieille Sibylle qui tire les cartes sur les mains et que j'ai consultée pour vous . . .

Lintilhac points out that the first speech makes Bazile a copy of Tartuffe. It also gives him a history which has no relevance to his role; the generality of a proverb is more consistent with his nature. Bazile's second speech is likewise corrected toward generality and omission of the Sibyl gets rid of a superstitious distraction. The same "accidents" seem more comical if thought to be physical or atmospheric.

28. Beaumarchais states in the *Lettre modérée* (1775) that he knowingly involved himself in the difficulties deriving from Rosine's admission to Bartholo, and congratulated himself on having successfully emerged from the embarrassment "en se jouant de la nouvelle inquiétude qu'il a imprimée aux spectateurs" *(Théâtre, p.* 160). Strictly regarded, this is justification after the fact.

29. Bergson, *Le Rire: essai sur la signification du comique,* p. 86. He cites both Kant and Herbert Spencer.

30. A long variant shows more clearly than any passage of the definitive version the affinity between Basile and Figaro:

Figaro *(pendant qu'on signe).* —L'ami Bazile! à votre manière de raisonner, à vos façons de conclure, si mon père eût fait le voyage d'Italie, je croirais, ma foi, que nous sommes un peu parents.

Bazile. —Monsieur Figaro, ce voyage d'Italie, il n'est pas du tout nécessaire pour que cela soit, parce que mon père, il a fait plusieurs fois celui d'Espagne.

Figaro. —Oui? Dans ce cas, nous devons partager comme frères tout ce que nous avons reçu dans cette journée.

Bazile. —Je ne sais pas bien l'usage ici, mais chez nous, Monsieur Figaro, pour succéder ensemblement, il faut prouver sa filiation maternelle, l'autre il ne suffit pas chez vous [?], je dis chez nous . . . *(Il met sa bourse dans sa poche.)*

Le Comte. —Crains-tu, Figaro, que ma générosité ne reste au-dessous d'un service de cette importance? Laisse-là ces misères; je te fais mon secrétaire avec mille piastres d'appointements.

Bazile. —Allons, mon frère, je suis très content d'agir avec vous, s'il vous convient, selon la coutume espagnole.

Figaro *(l'embrasse en riant).* —Ah! friandas! il ne faut que vous en montrer.

(Théâtre, p. 767)

This version, of course, brought discredit to Figaro's character through identification with Bazile. The partial identity is the principal source of the variant's humor, by establishing at once a visible diversity and a hidden resemblance. The affirmed identity is then developed through allusions degrading to both, and each one accepts the abasement. The two characters fix their price, and with equal skill and impudence each returns the other's refusals. The dominant tone of the final version could scarcely accommodate this sort of wit.

31. Lintilhac, *Beaumarchais et ses oeuvres,* pp. 247-50, points out that at one time the play was to have ended with a scene of gratuitous comedy. In it the "alcade," a kind of Spanish sheriff playing a role analogous to that of Brid'oison in *Le Mariage de Figaro,* wishes to arrest at least the servants of the household but would release the very man, Figaro, who had once made a cuckold of him. Part of the dialogue of this scene passed into *Le Mariage de Figaro.*

32. *Théâtre,* p. 157.

33. *Ibid.*

34. See Charles Lalo, *Esthétique du rire* (Paris, 1949), pp. 33 and 42. Also significant in this connection is Danilo Romano's remark *(Essai sur le comique de Molière,* p. 100) about Molière's characters:

Dans les comédies de Molière, cette incohérence inhérente au genre prend une signification nouvelle par le fait qu'elle est l'expression de l'incohérence du héros comique. —Celui-ci se compose toujours de deux êtres incompatibles et coexistant dans un même corps.

35. In an earlier version of Act II, scene 3, the count succeeds in kissing Rosine's hand without Bartholo's appearing to suspect his identity, a trick which renders Bartholo unconvincingly stupid. Inversely, in a variant of the final scene Bartholo reproaches the count for proposing a comedylike ending to their affair, that is, for destroying the theatrical illusion. He also consoles himself for losing Rosine by assuming that she would have deceived him, and thus the priority of avarice over love in his value system vanishes. Lintilhac, *Beaumarchais et ses oeuvres,* p. 247, furnishes still another variant in which Bartholo places money and woman on the same level, no precaution being too great to keep them both.

36. Bergson, *Le Rire: essai sur la signification du comique,* p. 152 and Gouhier, "Condition du comique," p. 301 *et passim.*

37. It is also the opinion of Beaumarchais. After summarizing the play in the *Lettre modérée* he continues: "Voilà le fond, dont on eût pu faire, avec un égal succès, une Tragédie, une Comédie, un Drame, un Opéra, *et caetera. L'Avare* de Molière, est-il autre chose? Le grand *Mithridate,* est-il autre chose?" *(Théâtre,* p. 157). And he concludes that it is the characters which determine the genre of a play.

38. See above, p. 22.

39. Beaumarchais himself seems to find the essence of comic action in a complicated intrigue and apologizes somewhat for having blended in *La Mère coupable* comic intrigue with the pathos of a *drame* ("Un Mot sur la mère coupable", 1797). It appears, however, that though complexity can be useful in facilitating introduction of incidents, it is not the essence of comic action. (See *Théâtre,* pp. 459-62.)

40. *Théâtre,* p. 159.

41. See René Pomeau, *Beaumarchais, l'homme et l'oeuvre* (Paris, 1956), p. 138.

Le Mariage de Figaro

1. In an earlier version the play opened with a song in Suzanne's honor, the work of Bazile and Cherubin, which was followed by a mocking commentary from Figaro, a tedious aside of no value to the action *(Théâtre,* pp. 775-76). Besides, such a beginning recalled too closely the first scene of *Le Barbier de Séville.*

2. See the observations of David Victoroff on the comic stereotypes in "De la fonction sociale du rire," *Revue d'esthétique,* II (Janvier-Mars, 1949), 34-37.

3. In a variant quoted by Félix Gaiffe in his *Le Mariage de Figaro* (Paris, 1942), pp. 71-72, Figaro greets Bartholo as follows; "Bonjour, cher docteur de mon coeur, de mon âme et autres viscères." With this the irony receded into the background to the benefit of an allusion more or less crude and consequently changed in tonality. Another variant, in the Pléiade edition, ends with an attack on Bartholo *via* his profession:

> Bartholo.—Que la rouge gratelle vous en paie!
> Figaro.—On reconnaît un bon coeur à ses souhaits.

In the final text Beaumarchais kept the same general intention but realized it indirectly through a reference to Bartholo's unfortunate mule, and the allusion gains in "polyvalence." Earlier this belabored animal had another usefulness. At one time the scene ended thus:

> Figaro. —. . . Ah ça! Docteur, pendant que je vais mettre l'autre mule à l'écurie, mettez-moi, je vous prie, celle-ci à la raison. . . . Elle est d'un entêtement!
> *(Théâtre,* p. 777)

This time it was Marceline who was the object of a somewhat banal insult. She was then much less sympathetic than in the final version. The speech, moreover, gains wit by the identification of "à l'écurie" and "à la raison" through the same verb. It is evident here that in the final version Beaumarchais strove to condense and refine without loss of comic effect.

4. We have passed over Marceline's approach, which is not at all amusing, recalling the obligations of Bartholo *(railleur fade)* and forecasting the denouement. In a variant she is cut off by a protest from Bartholo:

> J'irais, grison apoplectique, agacer risiblement la mort avec les jeux printaniers qui donnent la vie? Vous me prenez pour un Français.
> *(Théâtre,* p. 777)

The observation does not lack comic and humorous wit, but Beaumarchais sought in revising to reduce the erotic allusions wherever possible.

5. Several omitted speeches, not without some comic value, specify Figaro's character in certain respects and cast a more unfavorable light on Marceline:

> Bartholo.—L'épouser?
> Marceline.—En très bonne forme.
> Bartholo.—C'est-à-dire appuyée de quelques privautés.
> Marceline.—Hélas! Je n'ai pas même eu le mérite d'un refus! Il ne m'a demandé que de l'argent.
> Bartholo.—Que tu lui as donné?
> Marceline.—Prêté.
> Bartholo.—C'est la même chose avec ces messieurs. . . .
> *(Théâtre,* p. 777)

The "bonne forme" of which Marceline speaks is modified by "quelques privautés," the nature of which can easily be guessed. In addition, Mar-

celine frankly recognizes, to her own degradation, that she would have
refused those liberties only with a certain regret. She can still transvalue them into lent-out money, perhaps a more binding tie.

6. The scene once ended in a manner again damaging to Marceline's
reputation:

Bartholo. –Et cet amour que tu me gardes?
Marceline *(en riant).* –Heureusement que l'amour n'est pas comme le secret; il
    est bien mieux gardé lorsqu'on est deux.
Bartholo. –Fort bien, ma vieille passion; mais il y a du plaisir à t'entendre, et
    si le coeur a souffert par-ci par-là quelque brèche, au moins l'esprit est-il
    resté sain, agréable et entier. Je veux, parbleu, t'aider à l'épouser.
                                                             (Théâtre, p. 778)

Marceline's risqué pleasantry suggests that she is not indifferent to Bartholo. Her pun on two senses of *garder* strips love of the secrecy attributed to it by common propriety. Bartholo's reply is weaker. His appro-
bation breaks up the dialogue and abandons the theme. There was also a
moment in an earlier version when Marceline almost offered herself to
Figaro. This would have made the denouement of the final version impossible.

7. Variants attest that the scene was once conceived in quite a different spirit:

Suzanne. –Qu'il procure, Madame Orbèche?
Marceline. –Assurément, oui, Pimbèche, et qu'en forçant les gages, il ait sous
    la même clef son homme d'affaires et sa dame de plaisir.

The insults exchanged here are comical because of the sonorous resemblance which places the two characters on the same level, though Marceline's contribution relies even more on erotic laughter. The second
variant likewise simplifies the irony:

Suzanne. –Qui vous méprise beaucoup, Madame.
Marceline. –Me fera-t-elle aussi le plaisir de me haïr un peu, Madame?
                                                             (Théâtre, p. 778)

The irony relies upon the opposition of respectful address and amiable
tone and the literal meaning. In the final version Beaumarchais took
pains to make irony emerge equally from contrasting terms and tones.
He succeeded in exploiting all the devices at his disposal.

8. Jean Hytier, *Les Arts de littérature* (Paris, 1945), p. 68.

9. Jacques Scherer, *La Dramaturgie de Beaumarchais* (Paris, 1954),
pp. 172 ff.

10. The Pléiade edition offers the following variant for the end of the
reply: "et parce qu'il ne peut rien baiser à Madame il veut toujours me
baiser quelque chose" *(Théâtre,* p. 779). The laughable effect here is
based above all on the allusion, the precise meaning of which is left
to the reader to guess, and on the identification of *rien* and *quelque chose*

by the use of the same verb. The distance between the terms can be increased only by tone; that is to say, the text itself furnishes but a pretext for the comic. In the final version the elements of comic interplay are richer despite the appreciable reduction of erotic overtones.

11. Beaumarchais excised a passage in which Figaro, in order to avoid Marceline, went so far as to advise Suzanne to declare herself pregnant. This would have kept the play on the level of farce or *parade* (*Théâtre*, p. 779).

12. The countess is never alone with the page except during these few exchanges. There existed a version in which she was for a short time locked in the dressing room with him (see Scherer, *La Dramaturgie de Beaumarchais*, p. 81). Several other variants prove that her penchant for Cherubin was more serious than in the final version.

13. Two variants attest the care with which Beaumarchais weighed the degrees of sympathy which the characters provoke. In the text of the variant Suzanne remains silent. From the standpoint of stage action this is a blunder, but it puts upon the countess all the blame for the lie and the ill-founded accusation. Beaumarchais clearly tried to spare the countess this perfidy by later taking away from her the initiative of making the accusation. We quote the final lines only:

La Comtesse.—Soupçonner un homme dans *mon* cabinet?
Le Comte.—*Vous m'en avez* si sévèrement puni!
La Comtesse.—Ne pas s'en fier *à moi* quand *je dis* que c'est *ma* camériste!
(*Théâtre*, p. 780)

The variant does render more logical the count's question, "Rosine, êtes-vous implacable?" But it less completely expresses his repentance. By transferring the role of direct accuser to Suzanne, Beaumarchais made of her, according to the point of view, the countess' spokeswoman or the voice of the count's conscience.

14. Beaumarchais omitted a "philosophical" reflection of Antonio, provoked by Figaro:

Figaro.—Il dit des sottises maintenant.
Antonio.—Il n'y a que les muets qui n'en disent pas, et si ça vous déchire le retympan, vous savez par où que ce monsieur a passé. Crac!
(*Théâtre*, p. 780)

For once, the gardener succeeded in returning the insult to Figaro, who is not at all mute; in addition, he seems to suggest to him the way to escape the difficulty, unless it is a trap. Thus it is easy to understand why he takes care not to show the commission. In any case, his role threatened to become too important and his person too malicious.

15. Figaro once carried impertinence still further. The following is the suppressed passage which followed Figaro's "nécessaire":

Figaro.—. . . A sa place, moi, je ne dis pas ce que je ferais.
Le Comte.—Je te le permets.

Figaro.—Quelque sot!

Le Comte.—Je l'ordonne.

Figaro.—Instruit de vos faits et gestes et prenant conseil de l'example, je vous
solderais tous vos petits bâtards paysans d'un bon gros noble enfant légitime,
et puis . . . cherche.

Le Comte.—Insolent!

Figaro.—V'là-t-il pas.

                                                        (Théâtre, pp. 781-82)

This was certainly too gross for the final version. Once again, it was the
count who obliged Figaro to speak up, thus falling into the trap which has
been prepared for him. In addition, he insults his valet, as Figaro had
predicted in "quelque sot."

16. Figaro's speech beginning "Me feriez-vous un crime" was once
preceded by two sentences: "Assurément, vous prononcez. La justice est
la dette du magistrat, et tout client qui la réclame est certes bien son
créancier" *(Théâtre*, p. 782). The language is not comic in itself, but
thus introduced the rest of the speech was clearer. In the final version
the count himself makes the distinction between magistrate and individual,
pretending to a nonexistent benevolence on the part of the individual,
whereby he prepares a trap for himself. Figaro can then limit himself to
attacking justice only; it is his adversary who in effect aims the blows at
himself.

17. They were much longer originally and slowed down the action.

18. According to a variant, Brid'oison continued with the following
reflection: "Le mérite alors tiendrait lieu d'argent" *(Théâtre*, p. 782).
This reduced the satirical impact of the preceding sentence by obscuring
the correction of abuse by still greater abuse.

19. In an earlier version Figaro delivered a charge against the rapacity
of all the palace retinue. The approval of Brid'oison then became absurd
without any mask, except his stupidity, and the discredit thrown on justice
deprived the whole lawsuit of its meaning.

20. Several other litigations of a more or less burlesque nature were
once raised before Figaro's case. They were without any relation to the
action or the characters and seemed to be simply a means for Beaumarchais to display his verbal virtuosity.

21. The same is true of a variant in which the debate concerning *ou*
was longer, and references to music were mingled with more allusions
to literature.

22. He was originally more cynical, suspecting an illicit relationship
between Figaro and Marceline. His decision to marry his former mistress
was due primarily to the recognized merits of Figaro, which in the final
version are widely advertised by Marceline. To have put Bartholo's conversion on the stage, instead of in a passing allusion, would have contributed nothing to the comic.

23. Beaumarchais had first given the doctor's former housekeeper a
disreputable past, which she herself revealed in detail. She had passed

through many hands before coming to Bartholo, and thus his refusal to marry her, on the pretext that her youth was deplorably spent, takes on a different overtone. One sees also that the powerful voice of nature which Marceline invokes is also a richly ambiguous term *(Théâtre,* p. 785). Under these conditions, in spite of her affecting discourse on the servile state of womankind, it is surprising that she had three candidates seeking her hand at the same time *(Ibid.,* p. 788). In addition to the delay which they caused, these developments were damaging to the comic movement itself. The satire was close to being a sermon, and, conversely, Marceline's well-known wantonness precluded her return to the role of loving mother. To fit her for the revised play Beaumarchais had to undertake a major reconstitution.

24. The variants retard the action even more. The comic elements which they contain are the same as those in the definitive version. Figaro indulges in a play on *embrasser* similar to that on *caresser.* Two speeches which follow, however, contain a comic maneuver which was lost in revision:

> Figaro. –Et la coupable main qui a couvert la face de l'homme?
> Suzanne *(riant).* –Tiens, je la livre à la justice. *(Il la baise.)*
> *(Théâtre,* p. 785)

This was an entertaining reversal of values, but Beaumarchais likely found it out of place in the midst of the scene of recognition.

25. One variant supplies a still more developed and affected version of this reply, in which the personification of the abstractions is pushed to the point of pure allegory. These allegorical beings could not be comic except in caricature.

26. The variant stresses even more her probable culpability, since she refuses with some feeling to give the ribbon to Suzanne.

27. Probably to accelerate the action, which drags somewhat in Act IV, Beaumarchais suppressed the count's gestures as he pricked his finger on the pin which sealed the note. Such action did call attention to the importance of this feminine item, but gained nothing for the comic.

28. Eugène Lintilhac, *Beaumarchais et ses oeuvres* (Paris, 1887), pp. 248 ff., points out that the original of this quarrel was in an abandoned version of the last scene of *Le Barbier de Séville.* The compliments exchanged there were more ceremonious, outrageous, and farcical, the plays on sonority less:

L'Alcade. –. . . Ils sont fripons de la même bande.
Bazile. –Je n'ai jamais eu l'honneur de parler à Monsieur.
Figaro. –En effet, Monsieur, c'est la première fois que j'ai cet avantage.
L'Alcade. –Ils s'embrassaient, quand je suis entré, ils sont amis.
Figaro. –Amis? Nous? Je verrais Monsieur échiné près de moi que je n'en pousserais pas un soupir.
Bazile. –Nous? Amis? Que Monsieur soit pendu quelque jour vous verrez si je m'en afflige.

Figaro. — J'espère que Monsieur ne s'en offense pas, c'est seulement pour mon-
      trer . . .
Bazile. — Vous vous moquez de moi, Monsieur, ça se prend comme ça se dit.

29. Beaumarchais eliminated a few remarks which could be thought
tedious, but which also transformed the character of the scene. Bazile
was trying to argue his rights, which brought about the intervention of
other persons at the expense of the prominence of the principal contestants and thus reduced the intensity of the humor:

> Bazile. — J'ai de bons titres.
> Marceline. — Il n'en a point.
> Figaro. — Moi je dis qu'il n'en eut jamais.
> Don Guzman [Brid'oison]. — C'est ce qu'il faudra voir au Siège.
> Bazile. — Comment diantre est-il devenu si subitement amoureux?
> *(Théâtre,* p. 788)

30. The variant furnishes another version of this sentence: "Partout
où Monsieur est quelque chose, observez que je ne suis rien" *(Théâtre,*
p. 788). The fundamental opposition is there, but the temporal conditions
of the reversal of values not being fixed, the sentence lacks ironical value.
Bazile seems simply to give way to Figaro and to recognize his own inferiority.

The whole variant shows that Beaumarchais was earlier closer to
weeping comedy than he remained. Bazile, Bartholo, and Antonio, all
converted to virtue, were ready to marry Marceline. This gave Bri-
d'oison an opportunity to intervene again. Brid'oison, who first bore the
name Don Guzman, a transparent allusion to Beaumarchais' famous trial,
occupied for a time a more important position in the play than in the final
version. Beaumarchais brought him into the scene frequently, and as a
result of his mania for "judging" all possible cases and situations, satire
on justice was more intimately mingled with the intrigue than it is in the
definitive version.

31. From a variant it appears that Fanchette was not so naïve originally as she appears in the final version.

32. Variants show that the text was once longer. Beaumarchais eliminated several unrewarding awkwardnesses. For example, Figaro explained in needless detail just what pin is used. Marceline belabored him
with proverbs ("Jetons la maison par les fenêtres"), and pointed a moral
lesson, reproaching him by the way for a "philosophie insupportable en
bavardage" *(Théâtre,* p. 791). In short, Beaumarchais kept the characters in their respective attitudes but resisted the temptation to preach
or otherwise overelaborate.

33. The variants on the monologue show the work which Beaumarchais
did both of condensation and development. The passage ending "partout je
suis repoussé, was at first extended by the following sentences: "J'étudie
à Salamanque. On vante mon esprit, mes talents, mon savoir, et je ne

puis être percepteur au quart d'appointements d'un mauvais cuisinier"
(Théâtre, p. 792).

The depreciation of learning also reflected on society itself; the same
depreciation, combined with sneers at the count's standing, is resumed
in *la lancette vétérinaire.* That is, the comic theme was repeated in a
form more complex, more striking (the distance between the contraries
being greater), and closer to the action.

34. The rebuffs in Figaro's dramatic career were once more richly
illustrated. The passage corresponding to that in the final version was as
follows:

Une autre fois je fis une tragédie; la scène était au sérail. Comme bon chrétien,
l'on sent bien que je ne pus m'empêcher de dire un peu de mal de la religion des
Turcs. A l'instant, l'envoyé de Tripoli fut se plaindre au ministre des Affaires
Etrangères que je me donnais, dans mes écrits, des libertés qui offensaient *la
Sublime-Porte, la Perse, une partie de la presqu'île de l'Inde, l'Egypte, les royaumes de Barca, Tripoli, Alger et Maroc,* et toute la côte d'Afrique, *et ma* tragédie
fut arrêtée à la police de Paris, par égard pour les *princes mahométans,* lesquels
nous font esclaves, et nous exhortant au travail, du geste et de la voix, *nous meurtrissent l'omoplate en nous disant: chiens de chrétiens!* . . .

(Théâtre, p. 792)

As the old text continues it emerges that Figaro wrote yet a third play;
this was clearly too much. The variant belongs to a stage of growth in
which all the action took place in France; the change to Spain involved
considerable revision. Even so, Beaumarchais took great care to pre-
serve the fundamental opposition, which brings out the absurdity of the
interdiction and the enormity of means mobilized to suppress so small
a thing as a play. Likewise he kept the contrast between deference for the
Mohammedan princes and their little merit, and accentuates the latter
through their ignorance. The eliminations also emphasize the absurdity
of their power. Religion is scarcely mentioned in the final version. The
sole cause of scandal is the seraglio. The excisions, of course, condense
the expression, increase its nervous energy, and bring it closer to the
action—all advantages in a tirade of such length.

35. In the variant Figaro externalizes his misery still more: "Mon
habit plissait, de partout, mes bas devenaient trop larges, et mon terme
. . ."*(Théâtre,* p. 793). The precise detail became comic because of the
transposition, and this detachment shifted the interest onto the personage
instead of attaching it to the satire.

36. Similar remarks apply to the variant concerning the *chateau fort*
and Figaro's book, though nothing in the final version indicates that a
book is concerned. In the first matter Figaro is laconic and more humorous and ironic than in the definitive version: "chateau fort où pendant
six mois rien ne me manqua hors l'étroit nécessaire et la liberté." Concerning the second he is more explicit:

Mon livre ne se vendit point, fut arrêté et, pendant qu'on fermait la porte de mon

libraire, on m'ouvrit celle de la Bastille, où je fus fort bien reçu en faveur de la
recommandation qui m'y attirait. J'y fus logé, nourri pendant six mois sans payer
auberge ni loyer, avec une grande épargne de mes habits, et, à le bien prendre,
cette retraite économique est le produit le plus net que m'ait valu la littérature.

(Théâtre, p. 793)

Despite its length the passage is amusing, thanks to the comic reductions.
Fermer and *ouvrir* become equivalents. Prison becomes a hospitable inn,
the punishment a benefit, and more generally the evil and the good equal
each other to such a degree that finally the *retraite économique* is almost
an act of free will. Beaumarchais kept this phrase, which in the final text
has an uncertain allusiveness, though precisely ironical in the variant.
Similarly, the identity of prison and the inn emerges in *l'obscur pensionnaire* of the definitive text.

All the variants but one call for a common grammatical observation.
Whereas the definitive version develops the recital in the present, leaving
the circumstances in the past, the variants reversed the temporal perspective, placing the recital itself in the past by the dominant use of the
passé simple. Consequently, the final version links these memories more
to the real present of Figaro, which is that of the play, and also increases
its dramatic importance, whereas the variants establish a break in Figaro's temporal situation. This difference in perspective contributes to
the attitudes: the humorous detachment of the barber is more easily perceptible in the variants. Beaumarchais preferred to sacrifice that element
of the comic for a tightening-up of the action. The tirade was originally
threatening to become an independent humorous story, another action
foreign to the comedy.

37. In place of the terse "on me met dans la rue" of the definitive text,
which effaces the euphemistic nuance of "pensionnaire, " a variant supplies a more detailed explanation:

Je fus remis en liberté; je ne savais point faire de souliers, je courus acheter de
l'encre de la Petite Vertu. Je taillai de nouveau *ma plume* et demandai à chacun
de quoi il était question maintenant: l'on m'assura qu'il s'était établi depuis mon
absence *un système de liberté générale* sur *la vente* de toutes les productions qui
s'étendait jusqu'à *celles de la* plume, et que je pouvais désormais écrire tout ce qui
me plairait, *pourvu que* je ne parlasse *ni* de la religion, *ni* du gouvernement, *ni de
la politique,* ni du produit net, *ni de l'Opéra,* ni des Comédiens Français; tout cela
me parut fort juste et, profitant de *cette douce liberté* qu'on laissait à la presse,
j'imaginai de faire un nouveau journal. Mais, quand je voulus lui donner un titre, il
se trouva qu'ils étaient à peu près tous remplis par les mille et un journaux dont
le siècle et la France se glorifient. Je me creusai la tête: enfin, las de chercher,
je l'intitulai "Journal inutile" . . .

(Théâtre, p. 793)

Transfer of the action to Spain required several revisions in this passage.
Nevertheless, Beaumarchais kept *l'Opéra* perhaps for the droll effect
which this Parisian element would produce in a supposedly Spanish setting. It is more important to observe that Beaumarchais again keeps his

comic theme in both versions; the simultaneous negation and affirmation of liberty. The effect is more vigorous in the final version because the negation, always enumerative, is more nearly absolute there. He kept also the title of Figaro's newspaper, but whereas in the final version this derives naturally from the comprehensive prohibitions, in the variant Beaumarchais took the useless trouble of explaining the origin of the name. Amusing and ironical though this is, it is lost in the literary satire without a direct relation to the hero, and it also recalls too closely the monologue from *Le Barbier de Séville*.

38. A variant presents Figaro, after the suppression of his newspaper, in an attitude quite different from that of the definitive version:

Combien de fois, alors je me suis promené le cure-dent à la bouche et les deux joues gonflées, comme un gourmand qui souffle la surabondance, avec mon estomac brûlant et mon pauvre ventre exténué! . . . Lassé d'écrire et de ne point dîner, je recueille mes forces et j'invente une loterie bien plus ruineuse que toutes les autres. On l'examine, on l'accueille, on l'aurait reçue; mon malheur veut qu'on vînt d'en adopter une autre plus damnable que la mienne.

(Théâtre, pp. 793-94)

The transposition into terms of starvation, where to appear to have dined is more difficult to bear than hunger itself, does not lack in comic effectiveness and humorous detachment. But once again, this made too concrete the Figaro of the past to the detriment of the one in the play.

The last part of the variant shows the same defect as the beginning. "Lassé d'écrire, . . . je recueille mes forces" recalls "las d'attrister les bêtes" and "je m'évertue" of the final version, as well as "fatigué d'écrire" of *Le Barbier de Séville* (I, 2). Moreover, the irony and satire are not thrown into relief. In the final version Beaumarchais maintains the initial idea, that the wholly relative honesty of Figaro must give way before fraud, but the master stroke this time consists in covering rapacity with the title of honesty, reversing in appearance the scale of normal values.

39. In a variant the count cynically admits that he would love Rosine if she were not his wife *(Théâtre,* p. 794). Inasmuch as this remark is addressed to the disguised countess, one wonders how without change the present denouement could have been reached.

40. This series of scenes included several passages *(Théâtre,* pp. 795-96) which added little to the comic effect and slowed down the action. Bazile, instead of confining himself to the monosyllabic exclamations of the final version, indulged in comments alternately declaring that he did and did not understand what was happening before his eyes. This was done presumably to repeat Figaro's game in the trial scene and to double the echo, but the resulting ridicule lost its importance at this point in the play. The same is true for Marceline's explanation of how she happens to be where she is.

The question which Antonio addresses to his daughter, "Mais que faisais-tu avec lui dans ce salon, " deserves a remark. It duplicated the question which the count addressed to Cherubin in scene 14, and Beaumarchais preferred to transfer the gardener's words to the count. The page's response is of a different comic intensity, with a possible erotic nuance, from what one might expect of Fanchette.

The countess failed to conceal a note of anger, which may well have been prompted by jealousy, when she discovered that Cherubin and Fanchette were hidden in the same pavilion. In this variant she was again close to realizing the vengeance on the count—that she repay him in kind by becoming the mother of a bastard—which Figaro was once permitted to suggest for her (see above, note 15). This she finally achieved in *La Mère coupable*, with Cherubin as the begetter. Cherubin's attitude leads one to assume that the count's remark (I, 10) is justified:

> La Comtesse.—Hélas! il est si jeune!
> Le Comte.—Pas tant que vous le croyez.

Even the "innocent" Cherubin of the final version was once coarser and contributed to the play's eroticism.

Finally, Figaro, much like Bartholo in *Le Barbier de Séville*, was once made to hesitate before signing his marriage contract, as if he anticipated regrets.

41. In a variant on Act V, scene 12, Brid'oison once more offered the services of "form" when the count became convinced of his wife's infidelity, but he was repulsed as "maudit bavard ès lois" *(Théâtre*, p. 795). In the final version, when he is offered the opportunity to judge the entire affair, his remark is found, in the light of the variant, to have a different meaning. His comment was to have been the culmination of a series of futile attempts to intervene, and if the omitted variant had been retained, the comic effect of Brid'oison's final effort would have been the greater.

42. *Théâtre*, p. 243.

Bibliography

Aubouin, Elie. *Les Genres du risible*. Marseille: Ofer, 1948.

-------. "Humour et transfert," *Revue d'esthétique*, III (Juillet-Décembre, 1950), 368-87.

-------. *Technique et psychologie du comique*. Marseille: Ofer, 1948.

Bayer, Raymond. "De la nature de l'humour," *Revue d'esthétique*, I (Octobre-Décembre, 1948), 329-48.

Beaumarchais, Pierre de. *Le Barbier de Séville*, ed. Frederick H. Osgood. Boston and New York: Ginn and Co., 1913.

-------. *Théâtre: Lettres relatives à son théâtre*, Texte établi et annoté par Maurice Allem. Bibliothèque de la Pléiade. Paris: Librairie Gallimard, 1957.

Bergson, Henri. *Le Rire; essai sur la signification du comique*. Paris: Alcan, 1901.

Brunetière, Ferdinand. *Conférences de l'Odéon: les époques du théâtre français, 1636-1850*. Paris: Hachette, 1896.

-------. *Histoire de la littérature française classique, 1515-1830*. Vol. III, *Le Dix-huitième siècle*. Paris: Delagrave, 1912.

Chapiro, Marc *L'Illusion comique,* Paris: Les Presses universitaires de France, 1940.

Gaiffe, Félix. *Le Drame en France au dix-huitième siècle.* Paris: Armand Colin, 1910.

-------. *Le Mariage de Figaro.* Paris: E. Malfère, 1942.

-------. *Le Rire et la scène française.* Paris: Boivin et Cie., 1931.

Gouhier, Henri. "Condition du comique," *Revue d'esthétique,* III (Juillet-Décembre, 1950), 301-9.

Hytier, Jean. *Les Arts de littérature.* Paris: Editions Charlot, 1945.

Lalo, Charles. "Le Comique et le spirituel, "*Revue d'esthétique,* III (Juillet-Décembre, 1950), 310-27.

-------. *Esthétique du rire.* Paris: Flammarion, 1949.

Lanson, Gustave. *Histoire de la littérature francaise.* Paris: Hachette, 1930.

Lintilhac, Eugène. *Beaumarchais et ses oeuvres.* Paris: Hachette, 1887.

Michaud, Guy. "L'Intrigue et les ressorts du comique dans *Le Mariage de Figaro,* " *Mélanges d'esthétique et de science de l'art offert à E. Souriau.* Paris: Nizet, 1952, pp. 189-203.

Moore, Will Grayburn. *Molière, a New Criticism.* Oxford: Clarendon Press, 1949.

Pomeau, René, *Beaumarchais, l'homme et l'oeuvre.* Paris: Boivin et Cie., 1956.

Romano, Danilo. *Essai sur le comique de Molière.* Berne: A. Franke, 1950.

Scherer, Jacques. *La Dramaturgie de Beaumarchais.* Paris: Nizet, 1954.

Souriau, Etienne. *Les Deux cent milles situations dramatiques.* Paris: Flammarion, 1950.

Victoroff, David. "De la fonction sociale du rire," *Revue d'esthétique,* II (Janvier-Mars, 1949), 34-47.

-------. "Le Rire et le rêve," *Revue d'esthétique,* III (Juillet-Décembre, 1950), 265-73.